MANO & MELANI

A Hood Love Story

K. RENEE

Copyright © 2020 by K. Renee

All rights reserved.

No part of this book may be reproduced in any form or by any electronic or mechanical means, including information storage and retrieval systems, without written permission from the author, except for the use of brief quotations in a book review.

Chapter One

MELANI

A sharp pain jolted me out of my sleep, I cried out because the pain was just too unbearable. Mano was out of town on business, and we both thought I should come and visit my parents while he was away. He didn't want to leave, but this business trip couldn't be avoided. His biggest fear about leaving me is that I might go into labor while he was gone. His fears were now our reality. Just as the pain subsided, I got out of bed and walk down to my parents' room.

"Mom! Dad!" I called out to them as another sharp pain ripped through me. Holding onto the wall for support, the door to my parents' room flew open, and my mother ran out.

"Lani, how far are the contractions?" My mom questioned, while massaging my back.

"They're coming pretty fast, but I wasn't timing it! Ahhh-hhhh, mom, it hurts so bad," I cried, gripping her arm.

"I know, babe. We have to get you to the hospital." My mom was calm, and I believe that helped me keep it together.

"What the hell y'all doing?" My dad questioned, as he came out, rubbing the sleep from his eyes.

"Gabe! It's time! She's in labor!" My mom yelled.

"I knew it wasn't the damn food she ate when she was complaining that her stomach was hurting her last night. I should have just dropped yo' ass off at the hospital like I started to do," my dad fussed, shaking his head.

"Lani, stand right here, I'm going to get you some clothes to put on. Gabe, go get dressed and call Mano!" Mom yelled, as she took off down the hall to my room. A few minutes later, my mom came back with some clothes for me, guiding me into the bathroom.

"I know it hurts, Lani. We're going to get you some help," my mom said, helping me slide my pants on.

"I can't take this pain, mom!" I cried. She began timing my contractions, and they were about seven minutes apart. Once I was dressed, she ran out to go put her clothes on. Just as my mom and dad walked out, another contraction hit, and I screamed out.

"Ohhhhhh God, this shit hurts!" I screamed.

"Shit! Gabe, pick her up, she can't walk down those stairs

like that." My dad was looking around as if she was talking to somebody else.

"Who?! Mmmmmm mmmm, hell nawl, Gia! You know me and pregnant women don't get along like that! I'm sorry, but I can't help her," my dad responded, shaking his head.

"Gabriel! Pick our damn daughter up, and let's go! Nothing is going to happen; she's seven minutes apart. But we need to go, right now!" My mom yelled. Just as he lifted me into his arms, my water broke. I was in so much pain I didn't even care, but I swear the way he was acting I thought he was going to throw my ass.

"Ahhhhhh, hell nawl! Gia, I know damn well yo' heathen ass daughter, didn't do what the hell I think she just did?! Lani, I love you, but that was some downright evil shit! I'm not helping you or your evil ass baby," my dad fussed, placing me in the backseat of his car, and we were on our way to the hospital.

"Gabe, I can't believe you were about to throw our daughter." My mom shook her head.

"Hell yeah, I damn sure was. That shit is all over me, Gia. That lil' nigga, in their floating around ain't no telling what the hell he put in that damn water," my dad fussed, pulling into the emergency room. Once they got me out of the car and into the hospital, they took me right up to labor and delivery. My contractions were coming rapidly, and I felt like I was going to pass out from the pain.

"Mom, did dad get in touch with Mano? I need him here with me now. I don't want to have our baby without him." I was a complete mess. I knew Mano would be crushed if he missed the birth of his son.

"I told your dad to call him," she said, and Dad came walking into the room.

"Dad, did you speak with, Mano?" I asked.

"Yeah, he's on his way and nervous as hell. He just called me; he rented a private plane just so he could get here. He said the flight was a little over two hours. Did the doctor come in yet?" He questioned.

"Not yet, they just got her situated and said someone would be in to check her in a few minutes," my mom responded. About five minutes later, the doctor walked into the room.

"Ms. Thomas, I'm Dr. Niles, I will be delivering your baby. I did speak to Dr. English about your care, and she's aware that you're in labor. I'm going to check to see how far you've dilated," he said. My dad stepped out of the room while the doctor checked me out. I was so damn nervous and happy at the same time. My son was on his way and I couldn't wait to meet him.

"Ok, you're about five centimeters dilated. Were you having the baby natural or were you interested in an epidural?"

I know damn well he didn't ask me that shit. "I need all the drugs you can give me!" I know I was a little louder than I needed to be, but I need those damn drugs.

"I'm going to have the nurse get your epidural set up. We have a little time before your baby arrives, but I want to get you as comfortable as possible. I will be back to check on you in about an hour," Dr. Niles stated and walked out. I was able to breathe. At least we had time for Mano to get here.

"Everything is going to work out, Lani. You need to get some rest and be excited that your baby boy is on the way." My dad walked back into the room, and my mom told him what was going on. Kari warned me about the labor pains, but damn, I didn't know it was going to be this bad. I'm happy that Mano and I didn't wait around to get things prepared for the baby's arrival. Our wedding was three months away, and I couldn't wait to marry this man. Almost an hour had passed before they came in and started my epidural. Once the medicine kicked in, I was feeling a little better and was able to get some rest.

Chapter Two

MANO

I knew this shit would happen. I'm glad Gabe called when he did, I was minutes away from the hospital. I had been calling every twenty minutes checking on Melani until Gabe told me not to call his damn phone anymore. That dude was fuckin' crazy, but he was soon to be my father in-law. So, I guess I had to deal with all of his crazy shit. My life has changed on so many levels. Having my first kid, marrying my beautiful girl, and my growing business. It felt good knowing that I would have my wife and son to come home to every night. I made the right choice by choosing Melani as my life partner. Lil' mama was everything I needed.

"Bruh, everything is going to be alright," Quad assured me as we pulled into the hospital parking lot.

"I'm good, just a lil' nervous." When the car came to a stop, we jumped out, heading inside the hospital. Once they told us where to go, minutes later, we were walking into Melani's room.

"How is she?" I questioned, trying not to wake her.

"She's about eight centimeters dilated right now. They will be back in to check her in thirty minutes. She's been asleep for about twenty minutes now."

"Mano," Melani called out.

"I'm right here, lil' mama." I kissed her lips.

"I'm so glad you're here, I didn't think you would make it," she cried.

"I wouldn't miss this moment for anything in the world. I love you, baby girl." I smiled, pulling a chair up to her bedside.

"You shouldn't have missed any of the damn moments. Maybe she could have scarred your ass, instead of me. You better hope that lil' nigga don't come out with a crooked smile and a fucked-up frown. Because if he does, his ass can't come to my house. I don't do demon spirits, and I'm telling you the way he did me issa a spirit or two floating in his lil' ass. His ass is demon-filled, 'cause he damn sure ain't holy ghost filled," Gabe crazy ass said, shaking his head.

"Man, stop talking about my damn baby. He is a child of God. Besides, he has my blood running through his veins, he's gonna come out just fine," I told him.

"No, nigga, he is the child of Satan and gone come out doing the Crip walk," Gabe said, and we burst out laughing. Aunt Tay came running in the room like her ass was on fire.

"Ohhh thank God, I didn't miss nothing! Gabe, why the hell did you wait so long to call me?" Tay asked him.

"You should be glad I called you to get you away from them damn demon seed kids you gave birth to." This nigga was always talking about somebody damn kids. But I couldn't even be mad at his ass, he talked about his own kids.

"Babeeeee! I think the baby is coming! Get me some help!" Melani screamed, and Quad walked out to get help. A doctor and nurse came into the room and said they were going to check her. Gabe and Quad walked out of the room and stood by the door.

"Melani, you're fully dilated, and the baby is crowning. On the next contraction, I want you to give me a big push!" Dr. Niles said to Melani.

"Ok," she groaned.

"Ok, here we go. Give me a big push, Melani!" He stated.

"Argghhhhhhhhhhh! Oh God, I can't do this shit!" She cried out, and my heart ached to see my girl in so much pain.

"It's going to be alright, baby. I promise you the pain won't last long. You have to be strong and bring our baby boy into this world. I love you, and I'm right here with you," I whispered to her.

"I love you, too! Ohhhh shittttt!" she screamed as she pushed again.

"Alright, Melani, this is it. Give me one more good push, and you will get to meet your baby," Dr. Niles told her, and she pushed.

"You got this, Lani," Gia said to Melani as she held one hand and I was holding the other.

"You did it, Melani!" Dr. Niles stated, as he pulled our son out and held him up for us to see him. The way my heart pounded for my child and girl was some real shit. I couldn't fight the tears any longer. I have never felt this type of emotion in my life. I never knew that I could love another person the way that I love them. I would lay my life down for theirs, and I would kill anyone that attempted to cause them harm. I couldn't wait until this woman became my wife.

"I love you, beautiful. Thank you," I whispered, and we held onto each other, shedding tears of love and happiness for our son.

"Congratulations to you both," Gia said, wiping tears from her eyes.

"Thank you, mom," I responded, as they allowed me to cut the umbilical cord. We named our baby boy, Demano Michaels Jr. This was the happiest moment in my life, and I could only give thanks to God and my beautiful fiancé. Once they got Melani cleaned up, all the family came back inside the room to meet Demano.

"Awwww, look at him! He is soooo handsome!" Tay said as she admired her great-nephew.

"What he look like, Tay?" Gabe crazy ass asked as he peeped over her shoulder.

"Dad! Go meet your grandson!" Melani laughed.

"Lani, don't rush me to meet his lil' ass. I need to make sure the coast is clear, that lil' nigga might have a gun underneath his baby blanket," Gabe told her and burst out laughing.

"If he doesn't, you can bet his daddy do." I smiled.

"Ion even know why these people let y'all in they damn

hospital. Nurse, y'all know you just delivered baby El Chapo? I would scan his lil' ass before y'all take him into the nursery with all the other babies," this nigga said, and the nurse had the audacity to look at my son.

"Gabe! If you don't hush and come meet your grandson." When Gia started going off, he walked over to see the baby. I can't believe that I'm a father. It's the best feeling in the world.

Chapter Three

GABE

Gia and I were walking down the hall, headed to the elevators to go home and get some rest.

"Babe, I'm in the mood, and you know how I get when I'm like this." Gia looked at me, and I shook my head.

"Gia, we in a damn hospital. Ion got time to go to jail with yo' ass today! Besides, we got to get home and get some rest. You know Ma and Aunt Cynt coming later today to help us plan for this wedding," I told her.

"Come on, babe. We didn't get caught the last few times we did it. I can't wait until we get home. We are always trying out new places to get it in, but we never did it in a hospital," she said to me.

"Hell nawl, Gia! If our asses get caught up, we're going to

jail, and I swear I'm crying rape. You will be sitting in that muthafucka by yo' damn self. What will our evil ass kids say when they see their mama and daddy in the jail report!" I don't have time to fuck with my wife and her bullshit. She's always trying to fuck in places we shouldn't be fuckin' in. Now her ass was pouting.

"Urghhhh! Bring yo' ass on, and I'm telling you now if you start making all kinds of noises, I'm leaving you right the fuck there."

"I won't, I promise!" She smiled. We found an empty room, and as soon as I closed the door, she was trying to take her damn clothes off.

"What the fuck are you doing? Nigga, this is a hit it quick type of fuck. This ain't no damn lovemaking scene from the Young and the Restless," I told her ass as she pulled her pants down to her ankles. I pulled her close, kissing her lips, as she fumbled with my zipper to get my dick out. I rubbed my dick up and down her slit and slid inside with force.

"Ahhhhhh!" she moaned as I thrust in and out of her walls.

"Fuck!" I growled gripping her ass cheeks. The deeper I went, the more she threw it back. Pounding in her pussy was all that I could think about until we heard talking outside the door.

"Ohhhh shit! I'm about to cum!" She groaned, holding onto me and grinding on my dick.

"Gia, shhhhhh, somebody is outside the door," I whispered as I put my hand over her mouth to stop her moans. I stopped moving, but my wife was still sliding down on my dick, causing my shit to rock up even more.

"I don't care, just fuck me," she moaned, and I began pounding her shit to get this nut off.

"Fuck! God, don't let this good pussy get me into some shit! Amen!" I had to send a lil' prayer up.

"Ohhh, fuck me, baby!" Gia screamed out, and I wanted to push my dick through her damn voice box to mute her ass! But I couldn't stop fucking her because I was about to bust this damn nut.

"Did you hear that?" I heard someone say, just as both of us started cumming. Gia was damn humming and shaking like her ass was having a fuckin' seizure. This is why I don't fuck with her ass with this fuckin' in public shit.

"Gia, hurry up and put your shit on," I snapped at her, and she walked into the bathroom like she was about to take a shower and shit. At this point, I wanted to toss her ass out this damn hospital window. I used the sanitizer that was in the room and rushed out, leaving her ass in the bathroom.

"Heyyyy, what were you doing in there?!" A nurse yelled out, questioning me.

"It was a lady throwing up, and I pushed her into the bathroom to help her. Y'all might need to do yo' job, instead of asking me a thousand damn questions!" I said to her ass, and when she turned to walk into the room, I hauled ass to the damn elevators. Gia better bring her ass on. I made it out of the hospital, walking fast as hell to my car. I'm only waiting five minutes on her ass. After that, she was either gone get a ride by Philadelphia's finest, or by Uber.

A few minutes later, her ass came walking out of the hospital with a limp. That's what her ass get for always trying to get some dick. "Gabe! How you gone leave my ass like that? You better be glad I heard what the fuck you told that nurse!" She laughed.

"No, you better be glad I didn't leave yo ass. You could have cleaned up at the damn house. You in there acting like you were 'bout to jump in the shower and shit. I'm done with yo' ass and this public fuckin' shit! Yo' face will be the only face on the morning news! Then you don't know how to sneak and fuck, you always screaming and shit. If you can't handle this muthafucka, stop trying to jump on it," I told her, and we bust out laughing.

"Babe, we supposed to be ride or die in this shit together." She continued to laugh.

"Noooo, nigga, I will ride with you until you do crazy shit to get caught. Then I'm snitching on yo' ass for being dumb. One of us got to be on the outside to raise that heathen ass' daughter we got." I smiled and drove off.

When we made it home, it was almost noon. Gia and I was both tired as hell from being at the hospital with Melani and Mano. I must say I think they will do a great job with their son, and I was happy for them. But I wouldn't be me if I didn't fuck with them.

"Babe, I'm so happy. Our grandson is so adorable." Gia smiled as we got out of the shower.

"Yeah, I joke around with them about him, but he's a handsome lil' dude. I guess I'll let him claim me, but he can't be walking around calling me granddaddy. His ass gotta come up with another name. He can call me big homie," I laughed, crawling in bed kissing her lips, and pulling her close. I closed my eyes and was out the minute my head hit the pillow. A few hours later, I was awakened by my damn demon ass daughter, Malayah.

"Dad, I need some money. I'm going to the mall with Nila and her mom," she said, standing over me with her hand out.

"Layah, do I look like I'm sleeping with my damn money? Why didn't you ask your mom for some money? God didn't bless me with a come up for your lil' evil ass to do a take-down!" I fussed, giving her the money I had in my wallet.

"Yes, He did. You only got the money because of me and Lani. God felt bad and decided to help you out!" This lil' evil heifer had the nerve to say.

"Layah, get the hell out of my room before I take your ass outside and spray that damn devil off yo' ass with some holy water." I frowned. She laughed and walked out of the room, counting her money.

"Babe, stop calling my baby evil! She looks and acts just like you and Tay," Gia laughed.

"Whatever! She's always talking shit, Gia. Her lil' broke ass need a job." Malayah just turned twelve and acted as if she was twenty. My phone was going off and I saw that it was Tay calling.

"Yo," I answered.

"Bro, I found it!" She spoke with excitement.

"Found what?" I questioned placing the call on speaker.

"I found out how we can get ordained. We can take the shit online and get our certification that way," Tay yelled.

"Ohhh lord. Is this shit legal? Y'all gone have my baby walking around thinking she married and won't be. Because you two niggas done got some backdoor certifications," Gia laughed.

"Gia, you worry about handling the wedding planner and food. Tay and I got this shit over here! Tay, bring your ass over so we can get signed up," I told her, and we ended the call. I got out of bed and walked into the bathroom to freshen up. When my wife walked in to brush her teeth, I just smiled at her. I could never get enough of her. I loved everything about this woman.

"I love you, even though you gave me some crazy ass kids. With you, it always feels like the first time I met you. I knew you were going to be my wife the day I snatched your ass off that damn stage. I was too far gone. Thank you for giving me such an amazing family." I smiled, kissing her lips.

"Awwww, babe, that was so sweet. You are the glue that keeps us together and I'm grateful you snatched me off that stage. I would never change a thing about the life we have, and what we had to do to get here." I walked up, pulling her in for a hug. We took care of our hygiene and got dressed. Ma and Cynt would be here shortly.

"Babe, do you want me to cook dinner?" Gia questioned.

"Nahhh, you can order something. I'm sure Layah is going to eat out with her friend," I responded, just as the doorbell went off. Walking downstairs, I opened the door, and Ma and Aunt Cynt were standing there smoking a damn blunt.

"Nigga, why the hell you just standing there? Move yo' ass out the way," Ma said, pushing me out the way. Aunt Cynt put the blunt out, patting me on the shoulder, as she walked into the house.

"You know you two old gangstas gone need to stop smoking that shit soon," I stated.

"Nigga, the day I stop smoking is the day that casket drop. And when that shit drop, it better be enough weed in there to start a wildfire!" Ma bust out laughing, high fiving Aunt Cynt.

"I know that's right, and for my ass, it better be enough to start two wildfires!" They both fell out laughing, and I shook my head. These two were a damn trip, and I was ready to have some fun with them this weekend. The doorbell sounded off again, and I knew that it was Tay. I opened the door and she walked into the house hype as hell.

"Bro, this wedding is going to be off the chain. We gone get us some matching robes. I'm telling you this shit gone be lit!" Tay said, walking into the kitchen, giving Ma, Cynt, and Gia a hug.

"That sounds good. Ma is in charge of the invitations, and Gia hired a wedding planner."

"I can't believe Melani and Mano are letting y'all plan this entire wedding and marry them. I would have never trusted y'all asses to plan my special day," Gia spoke.

"Gia, we got this shit! Lani said she didn't care just as long as her day is magical," I responded.

"That shit gone be magical alright. I can't wait for y'all to see the invitations!" Ma smiled, sipping on her drink.

"I must say you spared no expense on the venue, having the wedding at the art museum is going to be a magical moment for sure." Gia smiled, just as her cell phone started ringing.

"Bro, here it is, the Universal Life Church. It says that it's completely legal, the cost is fifty dollars, and not complicated. We will be able to perform weddings, and it will be legal! Once I get this shit, I'm passing out flyers in the hood and marrying anybody that wants it for $49.99. I'm gone get in touch with some of these niggas from the good dick alliance and let them know I got the sauce!" Tay started laughing and gyrating around the kitchen.

"Hell yeah, that's what I'm talkin' 'bout the good dick alliance! I bet all them niggas at the fine nigga convention is a member of that shit! You can't be that fine, and not have some good shit tweenks yo' legs!" Ma and Tay burst out laughing.

"Grams, they be trying to get you, I swear. I got bit by the alliance years ago, and they ain't let my ass go yet. Got my ass walking around here like I'm bowlegged when I'm supposed to walk straight. Lawwwwd and my poor cousin, Love, that heifer always walking with a limp," Tay said, shaking her head.

"Well, I can understand why, that husband of hers is something to look at," Lai spoke.

"I can't believe this bitch!" Gia yelled.

"What's wrong, Gia?" I asked her, she walked back into the kitchen, pissed off.

"That was Melani's stupid ass grandmother. After all these years, she decides she wants to get in touch with me. She said she heard that Melani was getting married and having a baby. She wanted to know why she wasn't notified about any of this, and that she has a right to see her grandchild!" Gia looked over at me.

"Calm down, babe. We will figure this out with Melani," I told her.

"Gabe, that bitch is just as evil as her son was. I know she's up to some bullshit, and I'm not gone play with her about my damn daughter or my grandson!" Gia yelled.

"Ohhh, she can come out to play if she wants to. We got that hot shit waiting for that ass!" Ma stated, pulling her gun out.

"Damn right, she better go find another granddaughter to fuck with!" Tay spoke, agreeing with Ma. I'm not sure why Melani's grandmother has popped back up, but if she knows what's best, she will go back under that rock she's been hiding under all these years. Gia tried to include her in Melani's life, but this bitch said fuck Lani. I know this, I will put her bitch ass in the dirt over my child. It doesn't matter who the fuck you are, man or woman, I will murder your ass over my kids!

Chapter Four

MELANI

I have been waiting for this moment. To see Mano bonding with his son is such an amazing thing to see. He hasn't been able to take his eyes off of him. He told the nurse that he wanted him in the room with us at all times. When they took the baby to the nursery to check him out and to bathe him, Mano went with them.

"Babe, are you feeling alright?" He asked while placing the baby back in his bed.

"I'm ok, just feeling a little discomfort, but I will be fine. They said we will be able to go home tomorrow. They're supposed to circumcise Demano sometime today so that we will be ready for release. Are we staying at my parents for a couple of days, or are we going back to New York?" I questioned because I kind of wanted to stay at my parents for a couple of days. I may need my mother's help. I'm a little nervous about being a new mom.

"We can stay with your parents, give you some time with your family. But I need you to get rest, Melani. You just had a baby and I need you in good health. I will be home with you and the baby as much as I can, but you know I have to work. I won't be traveling again until after my birthday." He smiled.

"I'm excited about you being home with us. I love you, baby." Knowing that he was going to be in town for a couple of months had me very excited. Since Mano took the job, he's been going nonstop. My cell phone was ringing. Picking it up, I saw that it was Kari calling.

"Hello," I spoke.

"Lani! You had the baby. OMG! I can't wait to meet him, we will be coming to New York in a few weeks. Congratulations to you and Mano," Kari said excitedly.

"Thank you. We are both so in love with this little boy," I said to her.

"Awww, I'm so happy for you. Josh is coming home soon, and he wants to see us," she stated.

"That is great news, I can't wait to see him. We go home tomorrow, but I will send you some pictures of the baby." We spoke for a few more minutes before ending the call. I looked over at Mano and he was staring at me.

"What's wrong?" I questioned.

"Nothing, you're just so damn beautiful! Thank you for giving me my son. You will never know how much I love and appreciate you for giving him life. I have never in my life witness such an amazing moment. I can't wait for you to have my daughter next." He smiled.

"That is not the wave, baby, I'm not ready to have another one! That pain hits different when you're pushing a human body out. that was too much for me." He was laughing, but I was serious. I needed a few years before I had another baby.

The next morning, I was getting ready to be discharged from the hospital. Mano and I were surprised that they didn't keep you in the hospital long. My mom said it's normally a day or two. We had nothing for the baby here, everything was back in New York. So, my mom was on her way to come and pick us up, since Mano's car was at their house. She had to go pick up a car seat and other things that the baby would need for a few days.

"Do you think you will need help with the baby once we get back home?" He questioned, walking up to pull me in for a hug.

"No, I want to raise my own child. I know a lot of the women in our family have nannies. But my mom took care of us, with the help of my grandmother and I want to do the same with my son. I know we may need help when I go back to work, but for now, we don't need help." I smiled.

"You're going to be a good mom, lil' mama." He kissed my lips and went to answer his ringing phone. The nurse walked into the room and started going over the discharge instructions. I signed everything, and we were ready to go. About thirty minutes later, my mom came walking in the room with bags and the car seat.

"Lani, here is your bag to get dressed, and I will get the baby dressed," she said, and Mano walked into the bathroom with me to help me get dressed. About an hour later, we were walking out of the hospital. My mom's phone was ringing, and she seemed agitated about the call.

"Mom, is everything alright?" I asked her, as we headed back home.

"I'm good. Your grandmother called because she said she heard you were getting married and having a baby," she spoke. I was shocked to even hear her talk about my grandmother since she was adamant that she wanted nothing to do with me. The shit my biological dad said to me when I was younger was the end for me, and I wanted nothing else to do with him. As a child, that crushed my heart. I never asked for him or even mentioned his name again. I wonder about him from time to time, but I haven't spoken to him or my grandmother in years. I guess she's getting older and wanted to be a part of my life now.

"Wow. So, what does she want from me? Is she trying to see me?" I questioned.

"I guess, but that is totally up to you if you want to see her. I don't get down with the woman because of the way she treated you. I will support you if you want to see her," my mom explained, and I sat back in the seat thinking about what she said. I haven't spoken to Mano about the details of my father and grandmother. We pulled up to the house and guards were walking around the grounds.

"Grams and Aunt Cynt are here visiting for the weekend," my mom said as she got out of the car.

"Damn, I thought Gabe stepped up and got him a security squad," Mano laughed.

"Never, Gabe doesn't believe in all of that unless we have some real issues. Other than that, he handles everything regarding his family," Mom told Mano.

"I'm with him on that, I will be the one to protect my family," Mano stated, as he took DJ out of the car. My mind was on my grandmother wanting to see us. Now that I have a son, I don't want him to be slighted in any kind of way. If she's genuinely trying to be a part of my life, I will try with her. I stopped my mom before she entered the house.

"Mom, I want to meet up with her," I said to her, and she sighed.

"Alright, but you just had a baby, I will call her and invite her over," my mom stated, and we walked inside the house. My dad came down the hall with his damn UV light, and a damn weapon scanner.

"Dad, we don't have anything on us," I said, laughing at him.

"I'm here to check baby Chapo. I need to make sure he ain't got no shit on him," My dad cracked up laughing, running his scanner over my baby. When the scanner started beeping, my dad was looking at DJ all crazy and patting my damn baby down. Mano was holding the car seat, and DJ and his daddy both had the biggest smile on their faces.

"Mmmmm, mmmmmm, this lil' nigga holding! Why his lil' ass smiling like that?!" My dad asked, looking at the baby.

"Because his daddy always got him! Even from his crazy ass grandpop," Mano laughed, holding his gun in his hand.

"Gia, I told you we shouldn't have let her hook up with this hoodlum!" My dad yelled as he followed behind my mom into the kitchen. Mano and I were laughing so damn hard my stomach was hurting.

Chapter Five

MANO

We were having a good time hanging out with family. Lani had just come downstairs with the baby, and Gia was putting the food out for everybody to eat. Aunt Tay, her husband Sin, and their kids were here as well. Sin was a pretty cool dude, and we promised to link up on the business tip. He is doing his thing, but I think I can make him a more lucrative offer. We were already supplying him with our product, so why not bring him into the fold?

"Tay, you need to watch the seed of Chucky around your baby. That lil' nigga gone have her ass floating in y'all pool. He said he doesn't like the way she looks, and he would rather give her to me. I told his lil' ass I didn't want his demon ass or his half-demon ass sister. Because if she's hanging anywhere near his lil' ass, we know she got touched with something," this nigga Gabe said, and Tay was shaking her head, agreeing. I laughed so hard; I was damn near choking.

"Bruh, it's nonstop with that lil' boy. I told Sin if he didn't get his ass checked out, I'm moving in with Love and Law. I was taking a nap the other day, and ion know, I just felt something in my spirit to open my eyes. When I opened my eyes, this demonic lil' nigga was just standing there staring at my ass. This is what I get for not praying enough to the good dick gawwds to not let my ass get caught up. Now I have to deal with a good dick nigga, that produces evil ass kids. Ion need this type of pressure in my life," Tay said, and Sin was shaking his head.

"This is what I have to deal with all the time," Sin stated.

"Old lady, you got some money?" Lil' Sincere asked Grams.

"Ahhhh hell!" Gabe laughed.

"Who the hell you calling old, Lucifer?! Y'all better get this small pint ass devil. Lai don't discriminate. I will fuck a kid up in 0.3 seconds," Grams said.

"You not gone do nothing to me, my daddy got guns!" Lil Sin said to her.

"Sincere! Shut your damn mouth and apologize!" Sin told him.

"I knowww this lil' nigga didn't just threaten me!" Grams was pointing back and forth at herself. I was bent the hell over in laughter.

"Ion know what you heard, but I heard that lil' nigga say he gone get his daddy gun and take yo' old ass out, ma!" Gabe instigating ass told her, laughing his ass off.

"Lawwwd, this boy done threatened Grams. I give you the permission to beat the demon right on up out of his ass!" Tay said to her.

"This is why I don't mess with people kids. This lil' nigga gone make me stick my foot in his lil' bad ass. Lawwwd, chile, I need to smoke to get my nerves right," Grams said, just as lil' Sin ass stuck his tongue out at her. We all fell out laughing because Grams started chasing his lil' ass all over the house. I have never witnessed a family so damn crazy in my life.

"Ma, you might as well give the hell up. That lil' nigga fast as hell, and it looks like the front of yo' damn wig done got twisted to the side," Gabe told her.

"Yeah, it looks like one side of yo' head was in a gang fight! But I know how you feel, I be ready to straight close line his lil' ass at home." Tay told Grams, and I swear we all lost it. The doorbell sounded off, and Gia got up to go answer the door. A few minutes later, Gia came back into the room with a woman following behind her. Melani stood to go greet the woman, so I assumed it was her grandmother. She explained to me what went down when she was younger, and I was hurt for my girl. The woman didn't speak; she just stood there with this mean look on her face.

"How are you, Grandma?" Melani asked as she stood in front of her.

"You should have been trying to find that out years ago. Instead, I had to hear it from someone else that you were pregnant and getting married. Your father would be pissed to know that you haven't checked on me," her grandmother snapped, and I was fuckin' pissed.

"Joanne, what you not gone do is come in here and talk shit to my damn daughter. I thought you had good intentions on seeing Melani, but you can get the fuck out of my house if you're coming with this bullshit!" Gia yelled.

"Somebody better tell her, 'cause her crow mouth ass can get all these hollow tips! Wheeew chile, I hate a messy bitch!" Grams fussed.

"I know that's right, coming up in here like she got hit with a bag of bad dicks!" Tay added as she burst out laughing and high-fived Grams.

"Girl, she ain't never gone find out what a good dick fine nigga feel like!" Grams said, and they all fell out.

"This is what you raised her around, a bunch of hoodrats?!" Joanne angrily spat.

"Let me tell you something, don't worry about how we raised our daughter. You seem like you're here on some bull-shit. So, I want you to turn around and take yo' Tonka truck looking ass up out of my damn house!" Gabe was serious he wanted her ass out. I didn't appreciate how this bitch was talking to my damn woman. I don't disrespect women at all, but her ass was pushing it.

"Melani, you should have been woman enough to reach out to me. I see you've turned out just like your whore of a mother!" This bitch yelled.

"Whore, I got your whore, bitch! I will beat the shit out

of this lady. Y'all better get her ass out of my damn house!" Gia was pissed.

"I got you, sis. I can handle all yo work!" Tay jumped up ready to put hands on this woman.

"Nah, this shit not gone work for me. I don't know what your plan was when you walked up in here. You're coming in here talking to my girl like shit. Talk to her with respect or don't talk to her at all. You should have been trying to fix shit with your granddaughter, but instead, you wanted to be on some other bullshit. Well, let me go ahead and be the first to tell you. Fuckin' with my girl means you fuckin' with me. I don't disrespect women, and I hate to see other niggas disrespect women. Just know this, I will blow your fuckin' head off your miserable ass body over mine. One more thing, fucking with my mother-in-law will get you the same fate. She hasn't seen you in all these years, I'm pretty sure she won't miss your ass!" I told her, and I meant what the fuck I said.

"Well damn! This fine nigga gets finer with every word he speaks," Grams blurted out just as Melani walked up, wrapping her arms around me.

"Fuck you, you're a disrespectful ass nigga!" Joanne yelled at me, and out of nowhere, Melani hauled off and slapped the shit out of her.

"Ewwwww, what's that?! Gabe, you got a roach crawling on the floor!" Tay yelled with her nose turned up. When she said that shit, Gabe lost his damn mind! He started stomping the damn floor and running to his damn kit.

"Ion got no damn roaches! Ahhh hell nawl! Gia, you let her old ass in here without checking her ass out. Mmmmmm, mmmmm yo' ass gotta go!" This nigga started spraying the lady as he pulled her out the door. Her purse hit the ground, and Tay came out with a gun, pointing it at the purse and lit that bitch on fire! I lost it. I can't believe she lit this damn lady shit on fire.

"What the fuck are you doing?! I don't have no damn roaches! You're spraying me with fuckin' Raid, and this crazy bitch done set my purse on fire. I'm calling the police. I had my money in my purse. You need to go to jail for this shit. I know you and Gia killed my son!" She yelled at Gabe.

"You're lucky we didn't set yo' old ass on fire, bringing that bullshit up in my house!" Gabe was pissed.

"The fuck you thought this was? Coming up in here and you done came with yo' family members? Keep talking and I'mma set that half a wig you got on that damn crooked ass head of yours on fire," Tay laughed, and Gia walked up, handing Gabe something.

"You can believe what the fuck you want to believe, but for now you gone get the fuck off my property. Take this money and go buy yo' ass a new wig, bag, and maybe a new damn body. That shit you got is rundown and it looks like you could use a new one," Gabe told her. Grams, Tay, and Aunt Cynt were laughing so damn hard they were damn near on the ground.

"Wheeeww Chile, you can't make this shit up even if you wanted too," Grams laughed, bending down to light her damn blunt from the burning purse.

"How could she come over here acting like that! I never want to see her again, and I don't want her around our child," Melani spoke with a face full of tears as I wrapped my arms around her to console her. The way her grandmother treated her was wrong. I'm not sure what she knew about her father and all the shit behind his death. I decided that she's seen and heard enough of this bullshit. I pulled her inside, and we went up to spend some time with our son.

Chapter Six

GABE

That bitch has lost her mind coming up in my shit, just to get some shit off her chest! She didn't give ten fucks about making shit good with Melani. In my mind, she wanted Melani to think that we did something to her punk ass donor. One thing about me is I don't give a fuck what she has to say. I killed that nigga because he was fucking with my family. That nigga shot my damn wife; you damn right I killed him, and I would do that shit all over again. Gia and I made a vow that we would never talk about Tommy again unless Melani wanted answers. She never came to us about him and never asked for him after that day, so we never discussed it. Melani was my daughter and I would do anything to protect her.

"Babe, are you ok?" Gia walked into the room, sitting down beside me.

"I'm good, I'm just pissed off. I knew this wasn't a good idea. Has Melani said anything to you?" I asked because I knew she was upset.

"No, she went to her room with Mano. I think it's best that we allow her to process everything. She will come to us when she's ready to talk about it." What Gia said made sense. Gia and I went back downstairs to eat dinner since we all were disturbed. Something tells me that this Joanne bitch was going to be a problem.

"Gia, y'all better watch that lady. She gave zero fucks about coming in here starting her mess. It was something about her that made my ass itch. Let me know if you need us for anything," Ma said as she sipped on her drink.

"I feel the same way, I don't think we've seen the last of her ass. I can guarantee you this, she can get dealt the same fate her son was dealt with, and that's on everything I love," I said what I had to say about the matter.

"Bruh, you ain't have to spray that lady like that!" Tay laughed.

"Yes, the fuck I did. How you gone come up in my shit and you got them bitches walking around with you? That reminds me of that Moni chick when she had the shit on her. Fuck that! Ion know why Gia let her ass in here without checking her out? I'mma fix all that shit tomorrow. That shit will never happen again. Errrbody gone be scanned before they come up in here. Now I got to call the exterminator, ain't nobody got time for them lil' niggas running around up in here. Ion feel like watching television and them niggas come in here handing me the damn remote.

Fuck that! I'm ready to pack everybody up and go stay at my daddy house. Gia, ion even think I want this house no more." I wasn't feeling this shit at all. I know they think I'm crazy, but I don't get down with nothing that crawls and can gang up on my ass.

The next morning, I was up early as hell, waiting on the exterminator to show up. I called the company we used as soon as they ass opened up and even paid extra for them to come right then.

"Gabe, I can't believe that you're having this big ass forensic light installed over the door. It's going to make our house look ugly as hell," Gia fussed when she came walking downstairs.

"I rather it look ugly than to wake up with cousin Benny and Aunt Flo crawling on my damn forehead," I told her ass, and she walked off into the kitchen. Gia knew how I was, so I don't know why her ass came down here fuckin' with me. About an hour later, the exterminator was done, and the guy was finishing up with my special light over my door. I walked into the kitchen and sat down for breakfast.

"Tay said she will be here in a few. Y'all are supposed to start your online sessions this morning," Gia spoke as she sat my plate in front of me.

"Oh yeah, I forgot all about that. I'm supposed to take Ma out to deliver a few invitations later. Good thing, the sessions are only thirty minutes, but we do need to get started. I already got most of my speech together, y'all gone love it." I smiled. The shit I put together was priceless, and I couldn't wait for everyone to hear it. I just had to run it by Tay. We have to make sure we're on the same page.

Chapter Seven

MELANI

I was hurt over my grandma coming here to start shit with me and my mom. I thought maybe she wanted to mend our relationship and meet her grandson. Instead, she came in here with this fucked-up attitude, throwing shit at my mom, dad, and I. I don't know what she meant about my mom and dad killing my birth father. Once I heard him say all that negative shit to me as a little girl, I wanted nothing else to do with him, and I never asked my mom about him again. To hear my grandmother yell out that he was dead, and my parents killed him, shocked the hell out of me.

"Babe, are you ok?" Mano asked as he took a seat next to me.

"I'm not sure how I feel. My dad was a fucked-up person. He wanted nothing to do with me all because my mom was in a new relationship. He walked away from me over jealousy, and my grandmother wanted nothing to do with me as well. Not once did he reach out or try to contact me, I felt that he meant what he said back then. I was willing to give it a try with her for the sake of our son, but I'm good on that shit. She came here ready to start some bullshit with my parents. I'm not sure where she's getting her information from. To be honest, I never knew he was dead. I never talked about him again until today." I didn't want to come out and tell him, but I was kind of hurt by her actions. My heart ached just a little hearing that my biological father had died.

"I'm here for you. Whatever you need, I got you, baby." He kissed my lips and we cuddled up together. The next morning, I walked into the kitchen, and everyone was sitting around eating breakfast.

"Morning, baby. Would you like me to fix your breakfast?" My mom smiled. What I really wanted was for her and my dad to tell me what happened with Tommy.

"Mom, Dad, can we talk in the family room?" I asked, and they both nodded as we walked off to have some privacy.

"It's been bothering me all night; I barely got any sleep because I was thinking about what Joanne said about Tommy.

I know Tommy isn't a conversation that we've had since the day he said he didn't want anything to do with me. Joanne said he was dead, and that you two had something to do with that. Is what she's saying true?" I asked, and they both looked at each other.

"Melani, as a mother, you will do anything to protect your children. Things leading up to the day that he said those horrible things to you, and of course, what he said was enough for us to do what we had to do. Do you remember the day I got hurt, and you helped take care of me?" My mom asked.

"Yes, I remember. I always wanted to know why you were sick and had to be in the hospital." I remember that time so clearly. I didn't want to leave her side, I felt so bad that she was sick.

"Lani, the reason your mom was in the hospital, is because my car was shot up and your mother was shot in the process. The person was trying to kill me, but they almost killed your mom. That person was Tommy and he went to see your mother in the hospital. He thought she was unconscious and admitted that he's the one that shot the car up. The only reason he lived is that we were thinking about you. The next incident that cost him his life was because of what he said to you. The worst way to get a bullet is to fuck with my kids, and he did that. I'm sorry that you're the one hurting in the end. However, I did what was best for us as a family. He would have continued to do things to hurt you, and your mom." my dad said to me. I sat for a few minutes and thought about what they both said. I can't believe that Tommy did that to my mom, she could have died! I was pissed and hated him even more for what he did all because he couldn't have her.

"Mom, I'm sorry he did that to you and dad, thank you for being there to protect us. I love you both." I stood and gave them both a hug as I walked out of the family room and headed back to my bedroom. Even though Tommy was my real father, he was an evil man, and all that I was feeling for him is gone. It's time that we all moved on and live our lives.

Later that day, my dad, Mano, Grams, and Aunt Cynt were getting ready to leave and go deliver the invitations to our close family for the wedding.

I wish I could go with them, but Aunt Cynt promised that she would record it for me. It was so funny watching them plan everything for the wedding. I know some would say we were crazy as hell for allowing my dad and Aunt Tay to handle the details. To be honest, I was low key excited about not having to deal with it all. I was just excited to know that when it was all said and done, I would be married to the love of my life.

MANO

I'm happy that Melani and her parents were able to sit down and talk things out. When she told me what her real dad did to her mother, I was with Gabe. I would have sent that pussy to meet his maker asap. He would have never had the chance to say hurtful shit to Melani because his ass would've been dead.

"Ma, why does Trixie have to come with us? You know her ass gives me the itch. On top of that, her lil' ugly ass always staring at me. I feel uncomfortable." Gabe and Trixie have a love-hate relationship. We believed that Trixie had a thing for Gabe, and she loved him, but Gabe hated Trixie's ass.

"Stop talking shit about my girl, nigga! Besides, she is helping me with the invitation delivery." I looked at Grams and shook my head. What the hell did she have up her sleeves? I should have thought about this wedding planning shit more carefully. We pulled up to the gates of Truth's house, and Gabe put the codes in for the gate to open.

"I don't understand why you can't be normal like the rest of us and mail these shits. Ion really know how much a stamp cost, but I know that shit cheaper than my fuckin' gas." I bust out laughing because this nigga was loaded with bread and was always complaining about his money.

When we walked up to the door and Grams rang the doorbell, Trixie stepped up in front of her. The maid answered, and Grams told her we were here for Truth. When Truth came to the door, Trixie handed him the invitation pulling her gun out, letting off a shot! We all hit the damn ground except Grams and Aunt Cynt. They were too busy bent over laughing. I swear that shit sounded like a real gunshot, but the damn gun shot out black and gold confetti.

"Nigga, I thought my days were over! I thought the good dick gawds had come down and said bitch, that's enough good dick for you in this lifetime! Bihhhh, I think I low key pissed on myself." Tay was shaking her head, trying to get up off the ground.

"Ma! What the fuck kind of invitation was that?! Had we been in the hood, the Chinese store would have had a new dish on the menu, monkey fried rice! Y'all keep on, that lil' ugly hoe gone be a distant memory. She fuck with me and I'mma send her lil weird-ass to monkey heaven." I swear I almost lost a lung when Gabe ass said that shit.

"I'mma need y'all to get your ghetto asses off my property. Got my damn maid still in here on the damn floor," Truth spoke, looking at Trixie, shaking his head. This damn monkey was sitting on the steps smoking a blunt and swinging her damn legs.

"Trixie, you did that shit!" Tay told her as she high-fived her. I pray to God somebody recorded this shit.

"Ma, you need to come up with another way of handing these damn invitations out. I'm still trying to pull my heart from my ass and put it back in its perspective fuckin' place. I swear you and that lil' hoe play too damn much! Keep it up and I'mma burn yo' lil' greasy ass!" Gabe ass was still sitting on the grass, as he fussed with Trixie. Trixie blew him a kiss and batted her eyelashes, and I fuckin' lost it.

"Gabe, Trixie look like she came from the good pussy gawds! She might have that snatch back cooch. She gone give Gia a run for her money," Tay told him and bust out laughing.

"That's some nasty shit. She better take her lil' ass on and go find her another lil' monkey nigga to fuck with. 'Cause it ain't here, heifer. Gia will fuck yo' lil' ass up." I can't believe this nigga was really talking shit to this damn monkey. Truth shut the door on our asses about five minutes ago. We all got back in the car still laughing at the foolishness that just took place. Melani and I decided this morning that we would be going back to New York tonight. Tay wanted Gabe to go to North Philly, so they could get fitted for their robes to perform the wedding in.

"This wedding is going to be litty. We gone show our asses! I guess I will mail the rest of the invitations since y'all want to act like lil' girls. But I'm telling you now, Trixie is delivering

Juelz and Zelan's invitation the same damn way we did Truth." That shit Grams talking about is not going to turn out good at the Kassom residents.

"Hell yeah! Do it, ma. Just wait until I come up for the meeting next week," Gabe laughed. When we pulled up on the block where the lady lived, Gabe ass was ready to drive the fuck off.

"Tay, I thought the lady had a storefront business. I'm not trying to go up in nobody shit," He fussed as we stood in front of the house we were supposed to go in.

"Bro, I promise we good!" Tay told him, as she walked up and rang the doorbell. Gabe ass ran back to the car and grabbed his kit, and I bust out laughing. I hope this nigga don't start no shit in this lady's house.

"Well, we just gone make it do what it do!" Grams said, and we all walked in behind Tay.

"Hey, Ms. Glenda. Thank you for being able to make these robes for us," Tay said to the older woman.

"No problem, baby. Y'all come on in the other room, so I can measure y'all," Ms. Glenda stated.

"Ma! Where are you?" A lady yelled out.

"I'm in here with my customers," Ms. Glenda replied to the woman. A few minutes later, a girl came walking into the room. When she spoke, Gabe turned his head so damn fast. This nigga almost had a fit! Grabbing his damn kit, he was ready to put in some work.

"Gabe!" The girl yelled as she stepped closer.

"Mo! Don't bring yo' ass any closer or I swear you gone be

an extra crispy chicken wang when I'm done with yo' ass. Ma, you better watch out. This is the chick I told you I set her shit on fire." Gabe spoke as he held his torch gun up.

"You're the one that set my daughter's house on fire? Why would you do some shit like that? She lost everything in that house!" Ms. Glenda spoke as she held her chest.

"Mmmmm, mmmm, you need to be directing them damn questions to yo' roach-infested ass daughter! That shit needed to be burned down, she had enough money to get her some new shit. I'm getting the fuck out of here. I don't need you to make shit for me. You related to her ass? I know you got some shit crawling around up in this muthafucka! Tay, you can get yo' shit made here, but don't bring yo' ass next to me at the wedding," Gabe went on and on. I had to agree with my father in-law it was time for us to get the hell out of here. I don't do bugs. I mean, I'm not gone be extra like his ass.

"You a disrespectful nigga! I don't have no damn roaches. I had that one lil' problem at my house, and you burn my shit down!"

"One lil' problem, nigga. You had a marching band in one half of the house and a street gang on the other half! Y'all bring yo' ass 'cause my trigger finger itching." This nigga said, just as Grams grabbed his raid gun and started spraying it. Gabe ass took off running out of the house.

"It was nice meeting you good people," she said to them and walked out as if she didn't just spray raid in these people shit.

"Ummmm, ion think we gone need those robes, Ms. Glenda." Tay looked at the lady, shaking her head.

"Fuck that, this nigga gone get his ass handed to him! I'm tired of him talking shit to me and embarrassing me every time we cross paths. Bobby! I need you to come here!" This Mo chick yelled out as we were walking out the door.

"I think she just called her dude or brother," I told Gabe.

"Ion give a damn who she called, that trick should have called pest control. All these years and she probably still dealing with the same bullshit. Them roaches should be old as hell. Some of their asses probably done went off to college by now," he said that shit with a straight face, but Tay and I were in tears. Some nigga came running out of the house with Mo behind him. He halted his steps when he was met face to face with Grams and Aunt Cynt's guns.

"I think it's best that y'all pick a battle that you can win, 'cause this ain't it." Grams was on her shit today. Her and Aunt Cynt was always ready to get down, and I was with that shit. They hurried and went back inside the house. We got in the car and pulled off; this has been one adventurous fuckin day. I should have stayed at the house with my girl and son, but Gabe convinced me to ride with them. It was time to get my family and head back to New York.

Chapter Nine

GABE

Everyone had left and gone back to New York. Gia was so upset that she wasn't going to see her grandson every day. Malayah came downstairs with an overnight bag in her hand.

"Where yo' ass going?" I questioned her; she seemed that she was in a hurry.

"I heard you let roach nation infiltrate our house. I called uncle Truth and asked him could I move in with him." I wanted to drop kick her lil' ass.

"First of all, I handled it, and secondly, how many times do I have to tell you that Truth is your granddaddy!" I told her lil ass.

"You told me the same amount of times that you should've been telling one of those doctors that crazy people go see. Has anyone ever told you that you are crazy, dad?! I mean, I feel you on the bugs, but some of the stuff you be saying, it makes you seem touched, and that's not good. I love you, and I want you to grow old with mom, but I think we should 302 you and get you some help." She gave me one of those evil ass smiles.

"I think we should send yo' lil' demon seed ass back to your real family!" I always knew from the time she was born that her lil' evil ass had it out for me.

"Layah, uncle Truth is outside. I will see you in a couple of days." Gia kissed her on the cheek.

"Bye, cra-cra!" her lil' ass said to me.

"Bye, heathen!" I licked my tongue at her ass.

"Gabe, stop talking about my baby. She's all that we have left, and pretty soon, she will be out of the house." Gia pouted. She was sad that Melani was no longer in the house. I will be glad when all the kids were on their own. I plan on traveling with my wife a little more. We have always been so focused on the kids.

"As soon as she leaves, I'mma burn sage all over this house. Just so all the evil can go with her lil' ass. You know that lil' heifer talking about she gone 302 me, Gia. I swear I'm doing a living will, that heifer will not get her claws into my ass. I want Lani to have all the say as to what will happen to me." I be damn if her lil' ass has me sitting in a small ass room with a straight jacket on. I pulled out my computer, so I could look at the session that Tay and I had to take. We were supposed to do it yesterday, but we decided to just do it today. I heard the doorbell going off, so I assume it was her.

"Hey, bro, you ready to get this done?" Tay asked as she sat down on the couch.

"Yeah, I'm ready." We pulled the website up and signed into our accounts.

"Ok, the first question is. Discuss the Hypostatic Union and its implication of the last supper? Ahhh hell, ion really know what Hypostatic means." Tay looked at me all damn crazy.

"Don't look at my ass, ion know what none of it means. All I know is on the last supper Jesus wanted all his people there. They sat down and broke bread together and drank some damn wine. Now what they did after that? Ion know because I didn't get saved until last year." If she was looking at my ass for the answers, our asses was not getting ordained ever.

"Lawwwd, we were supposed to get saved! Ion think I got saved with the right Gawd. I got saved with the good d... Oh, ion think we supposed to cuss while we're talking about the lawd," she said, shaking her head.

"Tay, you first need to call him by his name, and that is God. Where the hell you get Gawd from?" This damn girl was crazy.

"Listen, when I pray, I pray to the good dick Gawds. I ain't really go to church like that. I know I ain't right, but this is what we're dealing with. Here is the next question, what is your method of personal discipleship? Lawwwwd, this is getting harder and harder. The only one I disciple is Love when she was going through all her shit with Law," this fool ass girl spoke.

"Bruh, ion think that's what they're talking 'bout. I think we need to go to church and figure this out or maybe we need to read the bible. Make sure you read it out loud at your house. Maybe you can cast that evil shit right on out yo' damn kids." We both bust out laughing. I know they ass got some devil in them, but I love them." Tay packed up her computer, and we agreed to be ready to do this by next weekend.

Chapter Ten

MELANI

I t felt good to be back home in our own space. We had some finishing touches to do with DJ's nursery, so we had to make sure we got it done. Mano promised that everything in the nursery would be complete in a few days. I heard our doorbell going off. It must be Steven, our floor concierge, bringing the lunch I ordered. Mano had to step out and handle some business, but he said he wouldn't be gone long.

"Steven, it's good to see you." I smiled as he came inside with the food to place it on the table.

"It's good to see you, Ms. Melani. Congratulations, Mr. Michaels told me you had the baby while you were away." He smiled, and I was happy to see my friend. Steven and I talked all the time. He was a lifesaver many days during my pregnancy. It didn't matter if I wanted food, a candy bar, or ice cream; he would be sure to bring it up for me.

"Yes, we're so excited to have our baby boy here. It's good to see you, and thank you for bringing the food up for me," I told him as I walked him to the door.

"It's no problem at all, just let me know if you need anything else." We spoke for a few more seconds, and he left. I went to grab my phone; my mom sent some different designs over for the wedding reception. They all were so beautiful. I really didn't know which one to choose. I dialed my mom up.

"Hey, Lani," my mom greeted, and I could tell that she was smiling. I could always hear the happiness in her voice when I called her.

"Mom, I like the second design. I think that would look beautiful with the colors we have for the wedding." I was excited that my mom was helping me with my wedding.

"Yeah, I like that one as well. I will call the decorator and let her know that we will go with that design. Lani, are you sure you want dad, and Aunt Tay to marry you guys? I'm not sure if y'all made the right decisions. These two damn fools are going to show out at this wedding." I knew my mom was nervous, but I was alright with my dad and Aunt Tay doing the wedding.

"Mom, they will be fine. Dad knows how much this means to me, and I know that he's going to show out. It will mean so much more knowing that he married Mano and me." I smiled at the thought of it all.

"Ok, if you're fine with it, that's all that matters," she stated, and a few minutes later, we ended the call. I finished my meal and went to go check on the baby. About an hour later, Mano came walking into our bedroom.

"Hey, baby girl. How did the baby do for you while I was gone?" He hovered over me, kissing my lips.

"Good, he's been asleep most of the time." I smiled, as he continued to trail kisses down my neck.

"How long did you say we have to wait to have sex?" He looked up at me, and I bust out laughing.

"Six weeks, babe. I know it's going to be rough, but we have to wait." The look he gave me let me know that he wasn't trying to wait.

"Lani, I can't wait no damn six weeks to be inside of you. I know you need rest, and you have to heal but six damn weeks is too long." He let out a frustrated sigh.

"It's going to be ok." I laughed at his ass because he was really stressed the hell out.

"How are you feeling about that whole thing with your grandma? I'm sorry that shit played out like it did. That lady had no good intentions when she came there. I knew there was no way I was gone stand there and let her continue to talk her shit. You're getting ready to become my wife. As a man, my job is to protect you and your peace." I knew that Mano was pissed about Joanne, and so was I. We no longer had to worry about her; she was out of my life for good.

"I think when DJ turns a year old, we will start looking for a house. He's going to need some room to run around and this penthouse ain't gone work. This was my life as a single man, I have a family now." I could understand where Mano was coming from. Something with a backyard would be great, but for right now, our son was only four days old.

"I agree, but for now, we can enjoy watching our son grow, your birthday and our wedding." I kissed his lips and decided to take a nap before the baby woke up.

Chapter Eleven

VERONICA

Mano got me fucked up if he thinks he's just gone kick me to the side for that lil' ugly bitch he with. I got time in with his ass, and I deserve to be the one reaping the benefits. The day I saw him riding in Harlem in a damn Bentley, I knew he had stepped his game up. Besides that, the streets talk, and I heard he was making big moves. That lil' young bitch gotta go. If she thinks that she's won, she got another thing coming. I was with him when he was just street nigga hittin' the block. I got something for that bitch though. She was running her mouth like she 'bout that life. I was playing it cool because the shit I was cooking up was going to rip both their asses apart.

"Veronica!" This nigga was always yelling my name. I never understood why the fuck he couldn't just come look for my ass.

"Why are you yelling?" I went off as he walked into my bedroom.

"Forget all that shit, your ex nigga and his girl had their baby. I ran into him earlier, and he told me. Then I talked to her when she ordered food. You do know they're getting married in a few months, right?" Steven looked at me, waiting for me to respond.

"Urrgggghhhh, that nigga gone really try to play me. Out all the shit we have been through, he gets this bitch pregnant and is going to marry her ass," I snapped.

"Yeah, they really living the life while you over here struggling. You just remember our deal. Once we get him for this bread, I want my two million, and you can do whatever it is you want." If this nigga really thought I was giving him this money, he had another thing coming. I had to play along for now, because I need him to help me out with my plan. Steven and I have been fucking around for the past two years, but we were not in nothing serious. The only person I wanted to be in a serious relationship with is Mano. When Mano and I broke up, it was almost a year before I saw him again. He might as well kiss his girl goodbye. The bomb I'm about to drop on them is going to blow their shit up in smoke.

"I got this; we just have to make sure everything goes as planned." I smiled.

"Just let me know what you need me to do." He walked up, pulling me into his arms. I knew he wanted sex, but I wasn't feeling that shit right now. My phone was ringing, and I stepped away from Steve to grab it.

"Hey, mom." I knew my mom was calling for me to come and pick up my daughter. Kemani would be three years old in a few months, but she stayed with my mom most of the time. I had shit to do and didn't have time to be taking care of no damn kid.

"Veronica, when do you plan on coming to see your damn daughter? It's been damn near three weeks and we haven't heard shit from you. Your daughter needs clothes and I need money to pay these damn bills. Why the fuck would you have a child if you didn't want to take care of it? Keep fucking with me and I promise you're not going to like my next move!" She screamed and hung up in my face. I loved my mom, but if she fucks up my plan, I will fuck her ass up. I guess I needed to go over, see my daughter and take them some money just to shut her the fuck up.

"That was my mom, I have to go over there. I will call you when I get back home." There was no way that I was leaving this nigga in my house.

MANO

Six weeks later:

"Mmmmm, baby, fuck me! Oh God, this is so fuckin' good!" Melani moaned as dug deep into her pussy, hittin' her spot over and over again. "Fuck!" I growled as she held onto me while the water flowed down on us in the shower.

"I can't get enough of this good ass pussy, baby." I began sucking on her bottom lip, feeling her gripping my dick.

"I'm abbbo.....Ahhhhhh... I'm about to cum!" She screamed. I gripped her ass cheeks, spreading them further apart as I thrust deeper and deeper.

"Fuckkkkkkk!" I released inside of her, and I swear I was ready to go again. We showered and began getting dressed.

Tonight, we were celebrating my birthday with my cousin,

Jah and Kari. I'm glad they decided to come up and spend some time with the family. We all have been so damn busy and working, but it's time that we relaxed and had some fun. Even though it was my birthday, I wanted to make sure Melani has a great time. She is killing this motherhood thing and I was so proud of her. The woman I met over a year ago isn't the same shawty I have in my arms every night. Growth is a muthafucka when you're learning and evolving from that shit.

About an hour later, Melani came walking out of the bathroom, and my heart felt like it was going to burst. This woman was fuckin' fine! Having DJ damn sure added some weight to her in all the right places. Her hips and ass were wider, and she still had this glow about her. I would always mess with Lani and tell her that she favored Megan Good, which was true. My girl had Megan's ass beat. Tonight there was no comparison.

"Babe, are you ready to go?" I knew she was excited about going out, but I would have rather stayed home. Ever since the doctor cleared Lani, I have been deep stroking her ass daily.

"Yeah. Let's get this shit over, so we can get back home, and I can slide back in between those thighs. Kari asked the nanny that helps with the Kassom family to come over and sit with DJ tonight and I was grateful. With the help of Kari, we were able to convince Melani to think about hiring a nanny for DJ. We would only use the nanny during the day, and we would take care of our son at night.

"You know I will never deny you, I'm so glad I'm taking birth control." Melani was all for birth control, but my ass was ready to fill her up with more babies. I guess she was right, she still had shit she wanted to get done. I wouldn't always be home with her to help, so I understood where she was coming from. About an hour later, we were walking into the VIP section at Club Velvet.

"Lani, you look great!" Kari said to her as she stood to hug her.

"Thank you, sis," Lani responded as I dapped Jah up and gave Kari a hug.

"Happy Birthday, bruh!" Jah held his glass out for a toast.

"I appreciate that." I dapped him up. The vibe in the club was crazy as fuck and I was loving it. *Gimme Brain by Travis Barker, Lil Wayne & Rick Ross* was blasting through the speakers.

"You guys have less than two months left before the wedding. Are you both ready for the big day?" Kari asked.

"Yeah, I honestly can't wait for the day to come." Lani smiled. Our wedding and becoming my wife is all she talked about. That shit had a nigga feeling good inside. I was happy as hell that we're in the space together.

"Why the hell are y'all letting Uncle Gabe and Tay perform the wedding?" Kari laughed.

"To be honest, I didn't want an old boring wedding and that nigga funny as hell. Melani and I are both alright with it, just as long as our ass is married at the end of the ceremony," I told them, and we all bust out laughing. The drinks were flowing, and we were all having a good time until this bitch Veronica stepped into our area.

"What's up, Mano? Hey Jah, it's been a long ass time since I've seen you." Veronica smirked as she spoke.

"Veronica, don't come over here with your shit. You know what the fuck it is, and you know I'm not playing no games with you. So, take your ass back to wherever you came from before you get embarrassed in this muthafucka." I wasn't about to play no games with her ass.

"Why the fuck are you here?" Lani jumped up into Veronica's face.

"Lil girl, I would pipe that shit down if I were you!" Veronica snapped.

"Sis, I don't know who you are, and I don't give a fuck. It seems to me that you came over here to start some bullshit. My sis obviously don't get down with yo' ass, that means we don't get down with yo' ass. It's in your best interest that you walk the fuck away!" Kari said to her.

"Bitch, you don't need to know who I am, so it might be in your best interest to sit down and shut the fuck up!" When the words left Veronica's mouth, it was over for her ass. Kari swung on her ass so quick, hitting her in the face.

"What was that? Say that shit one more time for me!" Kari gritted with her gun pointed to Veronica's face.

"Kari, let her go, baby!" Jah urged Kari to get off of her.

"If I hear that you started some shit with my lil' sis, I promise you your days breathing will be numbered." Kari let her go but kept her gun out. Security ran upstairs, heading in our direction.

"Mano, you're just gone let these bitches talk shit to the mother of your child, and wife like that!" Veronica spoke with a smirk on her face, just as security gripped her up.

"What? Bitch, you trippin'. I don't have a child with you nor are we married. Your ass is crazy, and you need to go get some fuckin help. I haven't been with your ass in over three damn years! Psycho ass bitch!" Jah stepped in front of me because this bitch had me heated, and I was about ten seconds from choking the shit out of her ass.

"Ohhhh, baby daddy, but we are all of the above. Happy Birthday to you, and I will see you soon." This crazy bitch pulled some papers out of her purse and threw it at me. Lani jumped across the table and started beating her the shit out of this girl. I pulled Melani off her ass. The guards grabbed up Veronica and led her out of the VIP section.

"Mano, what the fuck is she talking about?" Lani questioned as I opened the papers, and it was a marriage certificate stating that Veronica and I were married on August 18th, 2016. There was also a picture of a little girl, and the name on the back of it was Kemani A'leyah Michaels.

"What the fuck! I'm going to kill this bitch!" I roared, pulling my gun out and storming out of the club. I knew Melani was behind me because I could hear her screaming my name. When I made it downstairs, security said she had jumped in a car with some chick and left.

"Bruh, what the fuck was that all about?" Jah asked me, but all I could focus on was the hurt all over my girl's face.

Chapter Thirteen

GABE

Truth and I were on our way to New York for our meeting. We were supposed to have it a month ago, but Juelz had something that came up. "Do you plan on stopping by and seeing Melani and the family while we're here?" Truth asked as we pulled into Zelan's driveway.

"Yeah, I tried calling her earlier, but she didn't answer or call me back yet. I will try her again later, and I know we will see Mano at the meeting," I told him as we got out of the car and rang the doorbell.

"Hey y'all, Zelan is in the family room," Ari greeted us, and we walked into the family room.

"Nigga, I thought yo' ass was gone be ready by the time we got here." Zelan ass was laying on the couch like he had nowhere to go.

"I'm ready, I was relaxing until you slow ass niggas got here." Zelan frowned as he stood to dap us up.

"Ari, take some steaks out. I'm going to cook on the grill for dinner when we get back. Y'all can go put your bags into the guest rooms you normally sleep in when you're here," Zelan stated.

"Truth, since you're going up there, ain't no need for me to go with you." I laughed, handing him my bag.

"Nigga, you should have been taking my bags up!" He fussed. "Fuck all that. This nigga, Zelan, got about four hundred stairs to climb and ion like fucking with these house elevators." They both looked at me, shaking their heads.

"You know to be a gun-toting ass thug, you one scary-ass thug!" Zelan spoke.

"You know I don't give two shits about what you got to say. All I know is I'mma be a safe ass thug," I told him. We hopped in the car to head over to Juelz' crib. Walking inside, we greeted everyone.

"Columbiana, it's good to see you and Shaft," I said to Kari, and we all bust out laughing.

"Uncle Gabe, you play too much," she laughed.

"I'm glad everyone is here. Juelz, Meek, and Zelan, Trixie has something to give you," Ma told them, and I was ready to see this shit. She promised me that she would wait to give them the invitations to Melani's and Mano's wedding.

"Ma, I hope you not on no shit today with that damn monkey." Ion even know why Zelan said that bullshit. He knew Ma always had something up her sleeve, and I couldn't wait to see their reaction. Ma had to threatened Truth not to say anything, and I knew it was killing his ass. Trixie walked up and handed each of them the envelope. When they were reading the invitation, she pulled her a gun out, letting off a shot, and these niggas pulled their guns so quick. Zelan let off a shot, and Trixie ass jumped and wrapped herself around my damn leg.

"Ahhh, hell nawl! Ma, get this hoe off of me! This was not the damn plan!" I yelled. The harder I danced around trying to shake her off my damn leg, the harder this lil' ugly heifer held on.

"One day, one of us is going to kill her lil' ass, and today was almost her time to go wherever the fuck monkeys go!" Zelan fussed.

"Nigga, why the fuck did you let off a shot in my damn house? That bullet could have hit somebody," Juelz ass went off.

"Shit, I thought somebody was in here shooting. Ma, you can't have her ass going around shooting out confetti to a bunch of damn gangstas!" Zelan looked at Ma, and she was still laughing.

"Boy, I tell you. The older y'all get, the softer you niggas are." She fell out laughing again as she grabbed Trixie off my ass. Mano came walking in the room looking as if he was mad at the world.

"Nigga, what's wrong with you?" I asked him.

"Some bullshit that's gone cause me to kill a bitch," Mano snapped.

"What's going on with you?" He needed to just tell me what the hell was wrong with him.

"A chick I was fuckin' with a few years ago, came up to Lani, Kari, Jah, and I when we were out last night. She's claiming that we're married, and I know she's on some bullshit!" The shit he just said caused us to look at his ass twice.

"How is that possible? I mean, yo' ass would know if you were married." I knew this shit was about to be a bunch of bullshit.

"Exactly! We were together for five years. We've had many conversations about getting married, but she always said she wasn't ready. She gave me a marriage certificate, and the shit seems legit, but I know I didn't sign this shit knowingly." This nigga was pissed.

"Damn, you need to go down to the courthouse and figure this shit out. You and Lani already filed for your marriage license, right?" I questioned, thinking that maybe some shit would have come up then.

"Yeah, but nothing came up." He shook his head.

"I will have my attorney look into it for you," Juelz told him.

"Thanks, man, but that's not all. She said that I have a daughter and I swear the little girl looks just like me. I don't know how any this marriage shit happened, but if this chick had a kid by me and didn't tell me, I'm killing her ass. On everything I love that bitch is dead," he snapped, and I didn't blame him one bit.

"What did Lani say about all of this?" I asked him because now I know why she wasn't answering my calls earlier.

"She's pissed, she hasn't said shit to me!" Mano snapped.

"Damn, she over there fucking you up, huh? I will call her and tell her to stop beating yo' ass until we find out what's going on." I patted him on the back.

"Gabe, shut yo' dumb ass up!" Zelan laughed.

"Do you have the document with you?" Juelz asked him.

"Yes, it's right here." Mano handed the document to Juelz. We all went into Juelz' office and had our meeting. I guess when this was over, I needed to go and check on my daughter.

Chapter Fourteen

MELANI

This nigga got me fucked up. How the fuck you don't know that you're married to another bitch? I can't blame him for having a child he didn't know existed, but this marriage shit. Nah, I'm not feeling that shit at all. The doorbell sounded off and I moved quickly to the door.

"Ms. Melani, you called and said you needed some help." I called Steven up to carry my bags down to my car.

"Yes, I need you to help me take these bags to my car while I carry my baby down," I told him, as I pointed to the bags.

"Ok, are you going on a trip?" He questioned, and I wasn't in the mood to hold a conversation with him right now.

"No, just going to visit my parents," I responded. Once I had everything I needed, we walked out the door. He needed to figure this shit out, and I didn't want to be here while he was doing it. I couldn't believe what took place last night, my heart was crushed. I love that man and all I could think about is my wedding day. I wanted to be his first everything; the first woman he married and the first one to bear his children. Now, none of that would happen, because another bitch has given him both. I'm so glad he didn't come back before I was able to get out of there. It took me a few hours to get to my parents because of the traffic coming out of New York. I grabbed DJ out of the car and walked inside the house.

"Mom!" I called out to her.

"Lani, what are you doing here?" My mom walked downstairs to greet me. When she got close, I just broke down into her arms.

"Mom, everything is all messed up. Mano's ex approached us, handing him some papers saying that they were married and have a child. He said it's not true, but Mom, I couldn't stay there with him. I'm so angry, and me being there is not good for either of us right now. I know DJ is a baby, but I don't want us fighting around him ever," I cried, and she just held onto me.

"Ahhhh, they're back. I'm never going to get no sleep now. Lani, you have to control your baby with all that crying," Layah stated as she stomped back up the stairs.

"Don't pay her ass no mind. Come on, let's get you settled into your bedroom. Lani, I have to say this. You're grown now, and in relationships, you will go through some shit. It's not always gonna be peaches and cream, sometimes it's going to be bullshit mixed in the cream. If you love your man, then allow him to sort through the bullshit. Besides, y'all have a baby together, and Mano is not the type of man to just let you walk away. So, I'mma need you to prepare yourself for the storm that's coming and believe me, baby girl, he's coming. I love you and will always be here for you, but I want you to at least listen to his side and trust that he will fix this shit," my mom said as she took DJ out of his car seat and put him in his crib.

"I just need time to think," I told her, just as my phone started going off, and it was Mano.

"Ma! Cra-Cra is on the house phone for you," Layah yelled out.

"I swear this girl and her dad are going to drive me crazy," my mom said as she hit the speaker on my phone that's in my room. I burst out laughing because my dad and Layah were going back and forth.

"Layah, put yo' mom on the damn phone with yo' Annabelle demon seed ass." I can't believe my dad called her Annabelle. That was one scary-ass movie.

"That's why I'm going to haunt you in your sleep," Layah laughed.

"Gabe, Layah, will you two stop it!" Ma told them and I laughed. Dad and Layah are always going back and forth, and the shit was so funny.

"Gia, I'm telling you something is wrong with her lil' half-pint ass. You think she might be a grown person, but acting like she a kid? You know like in that movie the Orphan. Ion trust her, and I think we need to watch her lil' ass, Gia," my dad said, and I was damn near on the floor.

"Babe, if you leave her alone, she won't start with you. What's up? I was in the middle of something," Mom asked him.

"Have you talked to Lani? Her and Mano are going through something, and she left with the baby," he said, and mom looked over at me.

"She's here, I know what happened, and I think he should just give her some time to digest it all." Mom was right. I just need a little time away.

"I will talk to him about it. Juelz is looking into this situation for him. I believe him on this one, that's why I'm not giving him a hard time. Something with that shit isn't right. Lani don't need to make any harsh decisions until she has the facts. Truth and I decided to come back home tonight, I will see you in a few hours." Once they ended their call, she came to sit beside me.

I had a lot to think about, whatever is going on, something tells me that it's much more to this story.

Chapter Fifteen

MANO

When I got home and saw that Melani had taken my damn son and left, I was about to lose my damn mind. I'm not dealing with this shit. She's bringing her ass back home, and that's all I'm gone say about that shit. I would never do know foul shit like that to her. If I was married, I would handle my shit before getting into some shit with another woman.

"Look, man, I know you're upset, and you have every right to be. Lani will be fine; you know women get emotional over shit like this. Be thankful you had the woman that went to her mama and daddy house. 'Cause you know some women would have put a bullet in yo' ass, and cry at your damn funeral like they didn't do the shit," Gabe laughed. This nigga was always trying to find a joke in every damn thing.

"I know you said you were going to pay this chick a visit. Do you need us to take that ride with you?" Truth asked me.

"Yeah, maybe y'all can save me from killing this chick." I dapped them up.

"It all depends on where she lives at for me. If she lives in the hood, I'mma stay on this side of town until y'all get back," this nigga Gabe said and sat on the couch, grabbing the remote.

"Gabe, get yo' ass up and come on!" Truth said.

"Tru, I know that you're my daddy, but you don't have to yell at me in front of people. Mano, you know you can call him Granddaddy once you and Lani get married." I fell out laughing because this nigga sounded crazy. We all jumped in my car and headed out to Harlem to the last address I had for Veronica.

"Nigga, this don't look safe over here. I'm glad I got my damn kit." Gabe ass jumped out of the car with his bag. We walked up to the door and I knocked as Gabe looked all around like something was waiting to attack his ass. I knocked a few more times, and nobody came to the door. We headed back to the car and Gabe ass was so busy looking all around, his ass tripped and fell into the trash can, falling and knocking the shit over with him. A damn muskrat popped out of the can and Gabe ass lost total control. This nigga was straight geeking, trying to grab his damn bag and get off the ground. Truth and I were laughing so damn hard, I wanted to lay down beside his ass. I pulled my gun out and shot the damn muskrat.

"Hell nawl! That nigga tried to take me out. I should go back and set his bitch ass on fire. Truth, I think you gone have to take me to see somebody. I swear I felt that lil nigga crawl on me," Gabe fussed, as he brushed his clothes off.

"Gabe, that shit didn't touch you. He was just as scared of you as you were of him. Now get yo' ass in the car and sit the fuck down," Truth told him as we both were still laughing. I decided to go by Ms. Carol's house to see if she had heard from her daughter.

"This is her mom's crib," I told them as we got out and I knocked on the door.

"Who is it?" She asked through the door.

"Mano." A few seconds later, she opened the door.

"Well, look at you. She finally told you the truth," she spoke.

"Ms. Carol, is Veronica here?" She was too damn busy looking at Truth and Gabe to answer my damn question.

"Nope, her ass don't live here, but she need to bring me some money for this child. She said she was going to come by weeks ago and we haven't seen her. I'm getting too old to be raising another child, but if I don't, this baby won't have anybody to care for her," she fussed.

"Veronica said that I have a daughter, is that the lil girl that you have?" I needed to see this little girl.

"Yeah, that's what she told me. Y'all come on in and I will get her for you." She walked off to the back of that house.

"Nigga, if that is your daughter, you need to burn this shit down and buy them another damn house. Because this shit not working for me, nobody deserves to live like this. I know that there are less fortunate people out here, but yo' ass got money to help this damn lady out." Gabe wasn't even being funny at the moment. This place was not fit for anyone to live in, and I felt fuckin' bad as hell for this lady. She came out holding a beautiful little girl, and I swear I was looking at an exact replica of me.

"Hey, beautiful," I played with her cheeks and she reached out for me. I pulled her into my arms as she lay her head on my chest. My heart pumped at a rapid pace, and it felt the same way it did when DJ was born.

"Ms. Carol, can I come b

y in a couple of days and take you two out for lunch?" I asked her, I needed to get a DNA test done right away.

"I guess that would be fine, but can you give us some money for food?" Truth and Gabe were both pulling money out before I could get any out of my own pocket. We all handed her some money, and tears just fell from her face.

"Ms. Carol, I'm going to help you out, but can you please keep this to yourself? Don't let Veronica know that I stopped by or that we're going to lunch," I told her, and she agreed. I was so damn pissed when I got outside, I was fuckin' punching the air.

"Come on, man. Let's get out of here." Gabe patted me on the back.

"Fucckkkk! I can't leave them like that. I need to get them situated in something tonight," I told them.

"Do what you have to do. I felt bad by walking out and

leaving them, and it isn't even my situation." I'm glad Gabe felt that way, and I'm happy that he's actually standing by me on this one.

"We understand, man. Do what you have to do." Truth dapped me up. I walked back up to the door and knocked. Ms. Carol opened the door.

"Ms. Carol, please don't take this the wrong way. I can't allow you and baby girl to stay in these conditions. I would like to help you if you will allow me to do so," I said to her.

"I will take all the help I can get. Son, I only get six hundred dollars a month, and food stamps for me and this baby. The state only gives me three hundred dollars, and I get food from the food bank. Veronica is my daughter, and she should be ashamed of the way she treats me and this baby. You know I had my daughter when I was thirty years old, I'm fifty-seven now. I thought I would be able to rest and live a little, but I would do anything for that little girl. I've had her ever since she was four days old, and Veronica doesn't give a shit about her," Ms. Carol cried.

"Can you go pack clothes for you and the baby? Grab your personal items that you need; you won't be coming back here," I told her, and she looked at me for a few seconds.

"Oh God, you're the blessing that I've prayed for." She threw her frail arms around me and I can tell that this lady has gone many nights with no food. It took her about an hour to pack up her and Kemani's things, but she didn't have a car seat for her. We only had to drive about twenty minutes away, so we did what we had to do. I had a house in Harlem, and I decided that I would let Ms. Carol stay in the house. Once I got them situated, I dropped Gabe and Truth back off to their car. I ran to Walmart and picked up food, and other things that they would need. When I made it back with everything, Ms. Carol was sitting up watching Kemani sleep.

"You have a beautiful home, and I can't thank you enough for allowing us to stay here for a while. I've never stayed in anything this nice before." She wiped the tears from her eyes.

"I only stayed in this house when I didn't feel like driving home. I would like for you to stay here for as long as you need to stay. I only ask that you not tell your daughter about this place. I want to get Kemani tested, I need to know if she's my daughter or not." I decided to be truthful with her.

"I understand, and you should get her tested. You deserve to know the truth, and whatever happens, I'm with you a hundred percent," she stated as she began to put the food up. It was really late, so I decided to go home and get some sleep. The only thing on my mind was Kemani and knowing if she was my daughter. When I get my hands on this bitch, I'm fucking her ass up.

VERONICA

I was sitting here on cloud nine, the look on Mano and his bitch's face was everything. I found out that they were going to be at the club, because she told Steven all about it being his birthday and shit. I knew I might get into some shit with his girl, but I wasn't expecting the other bitch to try me. They did get the best of me, but I got the last laugh, and I'm gone laugh all the way back into my man's bed.

I was headed over to my mama's house so that I can dress up Mani and takes some pictures of me and her. I know he was pissed off about the shit I dropped on him last night. Mano was a hard ass, but he would eventually come around. Having Kemani with me was going to soften the blow. I think I'm going to go get her and bring her back home with me. That way, he can spend time getting to know her here, and I can work my magic. My mom was probably mad as hell with me, but as soon as I give her some money, she will be alright. It was a little after three when I made it to her house. I used my key to get inside this dump, and it was quiet inside.

"Ma!" I called out, and I got no response. I walked in the back and she wasn't back there. I guess her and Kemani stepped out to the store. I decided to go outside and sit in my car because this fuckin' house was gross.

"Hey, Ms. Mary. Have you seen my mama today?" I asked the lady next door as she walked out of her house.

"She left here last night with three men, I watched them from my window. They seem like some nice guys and yo' mama didn't seem like she was in no danger. So, I didn't say nothing to them." She shrugged her shoulders and I rushed to my car. I dialed my mama's cell phone and didn't get an answer. I tried calling her again, and she finally picked up.

"Ma, where the hell are you?" I didn't even give her time to say shit.

"I'm safe, that's all you need to know. You need to get your shit together, Veronica. You left me and Mani in that house for weeks with nothing, and I told you we were getting low on food." This bitch had lost her mind talking to me all crazy.

"You get money and food stamps; it's only two of y'all, how the fuck can't you live off of three hundred a month in food stamps?" She was always trying to act like she was damn starving.

"I don't make enough to cover my damn bills; you know I have to sell some of those damn stamps. I can't even get a job because daycare would eat that money up. I don't know why

I'm explaining shit to you anyway!" She was gone cause me to smack the shit out of her when I see her.

"You're explaining it, bitch, because you got my damn daughter. Just tell me where you are, I'm coming to pick Mani up. She's gonna stay with me for a while," I said to her.

"No, the hell she's not! This child is not coming with you until I know that you're gonna treat her good. I don't trust you, and I think you got some shit going on. I will call you so that you can speak to her, but you're not getting her," this bitch yelled.

"That's my fuckin daughter and I want her back. I swear when I see you, I'm beating your ass." I meant that shit, she knows I'm not playing with her ass. Just as I was getting ready to go off on her ass again, the call dropped. She don't have nowhere to go and no damn family, so she would eventually come back home. I wonder who the men were that she left with. I attempted to call her back, but she didn't pick up. When I got back to my house, Steven was waiting for me.

"Your plan must have worked, Melani left with bags and the baby last night. When he finally came home and saw her ass gone, that nigga was pissed. If you're going to move in on him, the time is now. I can add your name to his visitor log." Steven smiled, and I was happy as hell.

As soon as I opened the door, we walked inside as he pulled me into him, kissing my lips. When he unbuttoned my jeans and slid his fingers across my clit, I lost it. I pulled my damn clothes off quick as hell, and he did the same as he rammed his dick inside of me.

"Yeahhhh, yo' pussy tight as fuck!" He pounded in my shit and it felt so fuckin' good.

"Fuckkk, daddy! Fuck this pussy!" I groaned, as I gyrated on his dick. One thing about Steven is the nigga could fuck.

"Ohhhh shit, Lan... Ummmm, you better let that shit go before I cum," he groaned. I rolled my eyes because this nigga was always a one-minute nigga. How you gone have some good dick, but couldn't fuck past five minutes? I grinded into him, trying to get my shit off.

"Fuckkkkkk, I'm cumming!" I screamed as my body jerked.

"That shit was bangin," he said, slapping his dick on my clit. I was so damn irritated this weak ass nigga almost called me Lani. I knew he had a thing for Mano's bitch.

"I got some shit to take care of," I told him, 'cause I wanted his ass out of my house.

"I'm out after I wash up," he said, walking into the bathroom. I decided to wait until he was done to get in the shower. When he finally walked out, he grabbed his clothes and slipped them on.

"I will hit you up once I get your name on the list." He kissed my lips and walked out. I knew he had a thing for Mano's bitch, and he could have the hoe. All I wanted is my rightful place with my husband, and I guess our daughter.

Tay and I decided before we take the test to be certified, that we were going to church. Now we're sitting here in Beulah Grove Baptist Church.

"Tay, why you pick this church? Ion think these people want us here," I whispered.

"Nigga, ion know. The name just sound like they will pray the spuuurets in you even if you ain't got none," she whispered back and I bust out laughing. The two old ladies in front of us turned they head, frowning at us. Looking like Esther and some of her church buddies from Sanford & Son. The pastor just finished preaching and he said it was time for the communion.

"Bruh, what's that they're passing out?" Tay questioned as the tray was coming down our row.

"It's communion bread and wine. This is all about that last supper I told you about," I told her.

"Ahhhh shucks, so they drinketh in church. These lil' glasses too small, I'mma need a few glasses to feel anything up in here." Tay clapped, getting hype about the communion wine. After the pastor prayed, we ate the bread and drank the wine. I looked over, and Tay had four of these people communion wines, downing them one by one. The people on our row were staring and shaking they damn head at us.

"Ummmm, what the hel...I mean, can we enjoy our communion in peace? Ion see y'all watching nobody else, and Esther, you should be paying attention to the passa, not us," I said. These old women had my ass 'bout ready to cuss, and I know I ain't supposed to do that up in here.

"That's right. Gawwwd said come as you are and this is who I am. Now mind yo' business. Bruh, they should've put a lil' butter on that bread before they served it. That bread was bland and I'm still hungry." I laughed so damn hard; my stomach was hurting. I had to get out of here. The choir stood to sing and that was our exit song.

"Girl, yo' ass is crazy as hell. The bread was supposed to taste like that, and why you up in there drinking all them good people wine? You know I don't think that was wine. I heard some churches serve grape juice instead." I was still damn laughing as we got in the car.

"It was free, and the pastor prayed over it, I'mma be extra blessed. That's fucked up, if they fooled me and gave us juice. My ass wouldn't have, drank all that shit I would have just gotten more bread. I even got some bread for my damn kids. Maybe this will drive the devil right on up out they ass." We laughed so hard Tay ass was damn near hanging out the car. We got ourselves together and pulled out of the church parking lot. A couple of hours later, we had just finished taking the online classes to become ordained, and we passed.

"Yesss, brother! We did that shit." Tay's ass was dancing around the room.

"It says that we will receive our certifications in the mail," I told Tay as we high fived each other.

"Wheeew, I need a drink after all that hard work," Tay said as she poured us a drink from the bar.

"What are you two in here screaming about?" Gia questioned, walking into the room.

"Gia, you are looking at Minister Gabriel Thomas and Minister Taymar Williams." I smiled, and Gia was shaking her head.

"So, let me get this straight. You two have become ordained ministers, but y'all sitting here drinking like the sinners you both are?" Gia laughed.

"Gia, stop worrying about what we're doing. You know, since I'm a minister now you need to stop wearing them tight clothes. You need to go shopping and get you some first lady of the church wearing clothes. God sees and hears all things." I think my wife is going to make a great first lady.

"Praise the lawd, bro! Gia, go with Gawd chile. He knows your heart. We live by faith, not by sight! Without faith, it is impossible to please Gawd. Yess, lawd!" Tay dropped that knowledge on her.

"That girl good! You better say that, sister! Aman, and Aman again!" I cheered Tay on.

"Dad, I need some money," Layah said as she walked her begging ass into the room.

"Demon, I rebuke you in the name of Jesus!" I shouted, placing my hand on Layah's forehead.

"Daddddd! I still need some money you can rebuke me all you want." She stood there with her hands held out.

"Come on, Layah. I will give you the money; it's still coming from your dad." Gia grabbed her hand and they left out. Tay and I were set; we just hoped and prayed that it was still going to be a wedding. I felt bad for Mano, and I hope he got this shit worked out soon.

Chapter Eighteen

MELANI

I'm so fuckin' pissed and I know Mano's pissed at me, but I can't deal with his shit right now. My dad keeps saying that something isn't right with the story, and he's on Mano's side. He has called me so many times, but I just can't talk to him right now. The night all the shit went down, I tried asking him what the hell was she talking about, and he snapped on me. At that point, I didn't have shit else to say to him. I know emotions were high for both of us, but I'm your fuckin' fiancé, at least tell me something. The only thing he kept yelling was he didn't marry her, but there is a legal document that says otherwise. My phone was ringing, and I saw that it was Kari calling.

"Hello." I placed the phone on speaker.

"Lani, how are you feeling?" She asked.

"I'm pissed. I just want answers, and no one is understanding how I feel. How would you feel hearing that the man you're supposed to marry in a damn month, is married to someone else? He is acting as if I'm supposed to be ok with that, and I'm not. I hate that bitch, that's not her first time approaching us." The more I talked about this shit, the more I got pissed.

"I know it's hard, but from what I just heard, the document is real. My dad had it checked out, and it's in the court's records. The crazy part of this is Mano has no recollection of marrying this girl. Lani, I know this shit sounds crazy, but Mano isn't a man that will knowingly do some fucked-up shit like this. There has to be more to the story. I know for a fact that he's trying to figure this all out. I'm only telling you all of this because he told us that you're not answering any of his calls and text messages. The man is going off the deep end, and whoever is behind this better watch out for the storm that's coming their way." I guess I could understand what she was saying.

"I will reach out to him." I knew I would have to eventually talk to him. We do have a child together.

"Good. When this is all done, we gone get that bitch, believe that!" Kari laughed and we ended our call. I decided to go downstairs and eat while the baby was sleeping.

"Well, look who decided to join us? The runaway bride. Lani, you know when you get married, you can't run yo' lil' ass home. I wish Gia ass would run home to her damn mama. Especially if she leaves that lil' she-devil of a daughter we got. Mmmmmm mmmmm, bring that ass back here and raise yo' heathen." My dad was so damn funny, and my mom just let him say whatever. I loved the relationship they had.

"Dad, my feelings are hurt, and I just need time to process all of this mess," I told him.

"Lani, it's a lot to the story, and I was with him the other night while he tried to piece some of this shit together. That damn girl hid that lil' girl from him, and the living conditions she was in was fuckin' crazy. The chick wasn't even raising the baby; she left her with her mama," my dad said and I looked over at him.

"You saw her?" I asked.

"Yep, yo' granddaddy Truth and I rode with him to look into this shit. The boy is going through it, but that bitch should be ashamed of the way she left them. Mano felt bad and moved the lil' girl and her grandmother over to his house in Harlem. At least until he does a DNA on the little girl, but I can tell you this that kid looks just like him and DJ. I think you're gonna have a daughter to raise real soon. 'Cause ion think that baby mama gone make it," he said as started eating his lunch.

Damn, I guess I should have answered his calls, and I wouldn't have to hear this shit secondhand.

I just had the DNA test done on Kemani and I. They said it would be about five to seven days before I received anything back. I dropped them off and told Ms. Carol if she needed anything to call me and I would have Jah and Kari come over. I'm glad they were still in New York and was willing to help me out with them. I was on my way to Philly to get my damn family. I wasn't playing these childish ass games with Melani. I know she's hurt, but we gone deal with that shit as a family in our own damn house. I booked a room downtown Philly, and that's where we gone hash that shit out. Then tomorrow, we will come back to New York. I was almost at the house and I needed to talk to my mother in-law before I got there. I dialed her number, waiting for her to pick up.

"Hey, are you ok? I tried calling you a few times," Gia spoke into the phone and I smiled.

"I'm going to be alright, thank you for asking. I need to ask a big favor of you, can you watch DJ for me for the night? I'm about twenty minutes from your house and Melani, and I have some things we need to sort out." I was hoping she could do this for me.

"You don't ever have to ask me to watch my grandson. I'm not home, I'm out with Shanice right now but leave him with his granddad. I will be there in about an hour." Gia and I both knew that Gabe was going to have a fit.

"Gia, you know Gabe is going to show his ass," I said to her.

"I know and that's going to be the best part of it all." We both burst out laughing. I ended the call with Gia, and ten minutes later, I was pulling into their driveway. Walking up to the door, I rang the doorbell.

"I see you finally made it. She's up in her room, hibernating," Gabe said as he closed the door and I ran up the stairs. Walking into her room, she was lying on the bed and DJ was in his crib.

"Mano." She sat up.

"Put your shoes on, you're coming with me," I told her.

"I'm not going back to New York. If you want to talk, we can do that right here," she said with an attitude.

"I'm not playing this shit with you; you took my damn son and ran home to your damn mama. We not doing none of this shit right here. You wanna be mad, be mad in our shit! Go in one of the many rooms we have and be mad, but you not gone leave and come to another damn state. Make this the last time I have to come for your ass. I told you before I would drag your ass out of your mama and daddy's house. I'm not playing with you, Lani. Now put your damn shoes on or I'mma do that shit for you." I didn't mean to snap on her ass, but she had me tight as fuck right now. I grabbed her duffle bag, the baby bag, and DJ waiting for her to walk ahead of me. When we made it downstairs, Gabe was in the family room.

"I see y'all made up, that's good," Gabe said as he flipped through the channels on the television.

"Gabe, hold your grandson while I put these bags in the car." This was the only way that I was going to get DJ in his hands without telling him he had to babysit.

"Nigga, his mama standing right there. Hand his cry baby ass to her." He looked at me.

"I need her help," I told him as I placed DJ in his arms. This nigga was looking at my baby with his face all twisted.

"If you start all that damn crying, I'mma put yo' lil' ass outside." He told DJ and I was having second thoughts about leaving my damn kid with him. I eased the baby bag down by the couch and pulled Melani quickly out the door.

"Mano, we can't leave DJ!" She spoke as we jumped in the car.

"We are staying at the Four Seasons, and DJ is staying with your mom and dad for the night. Your mom is on her way home, and she told me to leave DJ with your dad," I told her as I backed out of the driveway. This nigga Gabe must have been on to us 'cause he came running out of the house.

"Hell nawl! Come back here and get this baby!" He yelled, holding DJ in the air. I drove off as if we didn't see or hear his ass. Both Melani and I were laughing because that nigga looked like he was about to go into cardiac arrest. I'm glad there wasn't much traffic out and we made it to the hotel in under thirty minutes. Melani didn't say much on the way here. When we walked into the room, she sat on the couch and was still giving me the silent treatment.

"Listen, I know you're upset. Hell, I'm pissed off about this shit too. Veronica is a conniving ass bitch and I'm gone deal with her ass. We're about to get married and as my girl, you can't believe everything you see and hear. She wants us to fall apart; that's her fuckin plan, and you letting her ass win. I never married this girl, and I knew nothing about her having a baby. Once we split up, I was done with her ass. I wanted nothing else to do with her. If I knew she was pregnant I would have been there for my child. Lani, you should have seen the bullshit conditions they were living in. That bitch left her four-day old child with her mama. I would have never allowed that shit to happen. I moved the baby and her grandmother into my house in Harlem. I took the DNA test earlier today, and if Kemani turns out to be my daughter, we will raise her. Because her bitch ass mama gone be dead and that's on me! I love you from the deepest part of me, shawty. I just need you to rock this shit out with me and know that I would never do you wrong." I pulled her up from the couch, wiping the tears away from her eyes.

"If you didn't marry her, how is this all legal?" She asked, and that is something that I have been asking myself.

"I have no idea, Juelz is helping me figure this shit out. His lawyer found out that the courts had the marriage certificate on file. I didn't marry her willingly, so the only thing that we could think of is that she knows someone that works there. I gave him all of her friend's names, and his lawyer is checking to see if any of them works for the city, or state. I should hear something back about that in a day or so," I said to her, hoping that she would ease up.

"I'm sorry. I was just so hurt, and when you yelled at me, I just shut down," she cried.

"I'm sorry for yelling, baby, but you have to understand that bitch dropped a bomb on me that night. I will never intentionally hurt you; I love you too much." I kissed her lips. I needed to be inside of my girl and relieve all of this fuckin' stress I had on me. I latched onto her lips as I tried to rip her damn clothes off of her ass. Spreading her legs apart, she moaned into my mouth, caused my dick to jump. I slid my fingers inside of her pussy, and that shit felt like a heartbeat thumping. When you use to getting dicked down daily, I know her pussy felt deprived.

"Ahhh baby," she moaned. I pushed her down on the couch, pulling her body to the edge as I kneeled down, gripping both ass cheeks apart. Diving in headfirst, I tried to suck every part of her soul out of her body. Moving my tongue in a circular motion and then latching onto her clit caused her to cry out. "Fuckkkkkk!" She screamed, and she was cumming a few minutes later. I wasted no time sliding inside of her with urgency. The way her pussy gripped my dick, I knew we were going to be here all night fuckin' all over this damn room.

"Got damn, this some good ass pussy!" I growled as I thrust deep inside of her, and Lani was creaming all over the place.

"Yesssss, baby, give it to me. I need you so bad! Ohhh shit!" She moaned, gyrating her body, trying to meet me thrust for thrust. Every time I slammed inside of her, I was trying to knock her insides loose. That's how bad I needed and wanted this damn girl. I felt her pussy gripping my dick again, and I knew she was about to cum. I pulled out of her, placed my mouth over her pussy and sucked that cum right on out of her. My baby was shaking and squirming, trying to get away from me as I slammed back inside of her.

"Stop moving and take this dick, Lani!" I growled. It felt like my soul was leaving my body, and I was having an out of body experience. I bust so damn hard inside of her walls, it felt like a damn explosion had taken place.

"Urgggggghhhhh, fuckkkkk!" I roared as I emptied everything I had inside of her. It took us a few minutes to gain our composure. I could only pray that things worked out for my family in the days to come.

Chapter Twenty

GABE

I was gone cuss these niggas out when I see their ass. Leaving me here by my damn self with this small ass gang leader. His ass was either crying or looking at my ass funny. That shit had me fucking nervous. You couldn't trust lil' niggas when they looked at you side damn ways. Baby or not, I didn't trust his lil' ass! I called Gia and she kept sending me to voicemail, and his mama and dumb ass daddy didn't answer the phone. I laid him in his swing while I went to go fix me a sandwich. By the time I got back into the family room, he was sleep. I was glad about that shit. I hope his ass stayed sleep until somebody came here. Layah came walking in the room and I forgot her ass was even here.

"Layah, take that lil' baby outta here so I can watch television in peace," I told her.

"Who?! I'm not watching him, I'm just a kid, and I'm

about to leave. My friend's mom is about to come and pick me up for a sleepover. You're not even fit to watch a baby; they should have taken their baby with them." This lil' greasy looking heifer had the nerve to say.

"You know, Layah. You were really adopted, and I think it's time we send yo' ass back to your real family. I heard it's hot where they live, so you don't have to take a lot of clothes with you," I laughed.

"Dad, I look exactly like you, so there's no denying me and if you tried, me and mommy are gonna take you to child support court and get all of your money!" She licked her tongue at me, walking out and slammed the front door. The baby started screaming and I know that lil' heifer did that shit on purpose. I called Tay ass over here and her ass was taking too damn long. I walked over and looked down at him, trying to talk to him, but that shit wasn't working. I picked him up, and the smell that hit my nose made my ass want to throw his ass back in the swing. I dialed Truth up to see if he would come over here.

"Yeah." His ass sounded like he was asleep.

"Tru, I need you to come over here and change yo' great-grandson diaper," I spoke.

"Nigga, I'm not bringing my ass over there to change no damn diaper. You change his diaper. Wait a minute, why do you have the baby?" He questioned me like I the fuck knew why I had him.

"Nigga, they just ran out of here and left this baby on me. Ion really change diapers and this nigga smell like death two times over. Now come over here and help this lil' nigga out. He smell like he needs a new ass. Ion think he gone want to keep the same ass after what he's going through in this paper," I said to him.

"Change that baby. How the fuck would you like it if somebody left shit on your ass? That's why he's doing all that damn crying. Change him, or I'mma shoot yo' ass when I see you!" He yelled and hung up the phone. That nigga was always so damn moody. I picked the baby up and took him to the couch, grabbing the pamper out of his bag. I undid the pamper, and I wanted to pinch the damn smile he had right off his lil' stank ass. Just as I grabbed the wipe, this lil' nigga had poop coming out of his ass, and I damn near threw up my damn lunch. It was too much going on, so I grabbed him holding him far away from my ass. I walked him out on the patio, so I could hose his lil' ass down. Just as I grabbed the water hose, Tay came walking outside.

"Bro, what the hell you doing to that baby? Ohhhhh lawwdddd, I know you not 'bout to drown that baby. He really don't have the lil' devil running inside of him lawd. Gawwd, I come to you as a recovering hoe! Please forgive my brother in his craziest times, oh lawd. He know not 'cause he asked not. He just a little touched, lawd gawd. With a lil' more of yo' guidance, he can be made whole. I ask that you come down right now, Gawd, and lay yo' hands on his crazy ass! In all these things, we pray. Amen." This heifer had the nerve to be praying and calling me crazy, but her ass was down on her damn knees, looking crazy as hell.

"Nigga, I'm not trying to drown his lil' ass. I need to get this poop off of him," I said to her with my nose scrunched up because this lil' nigga was stank. He wasn't even crying anymore; he was just smiling.

"Gabriel damn Thomas! I swear I'mma fuck you up, what the hell are you doing?" Gia yelled as she walked up, taking the baby from me going back in the house.

"Gia, his ass is full of shit, literally! I was about to spray it off of his ass," I laughed.

"You could have taken him in the bathroom, stay yo' ass over there away from him. Gone have our poor grandson scarred for life," Gia fussed, but shit, that lil' nigga was gone have my nose scarred for life.

"The next time y'all will know not to leave me to babysit until he turns ten," I said to her and she walked out to go clean the baby up.

"Bruh, you can't be scaring my ass like that. I was praying hard as hell that the good man above reached through yo' craziness." I burst out laughing because this girl was on her third drink.

Chapter Twenty-One

MELANI

We were sitting here listing to my dad go on and on about us leaving our baby with him.

"Y'all might as well get ready, 'cause I called the people on y'all for child endangerment. I know y'all ass saw me and Baby Chapo running after y'all too. God should be careful who He allows to have children. Ion really think y'all it, but we gone see when the people get here," he said with a serious face.

"Well, God should have really been careful when he gave you some kids. Thank God we have mom, or we would be a mess," my sister Layah blurted out as she walked into the kitchen. Dad damn near broke his neck to look at her.

"Layah, did anybody ask yo' gooseneck ass anything?" My dad loved going back and forth with Layah.

"Never leave my grandson with his granddad again. The

baby pooped in his pamper, and your damn daddy was about to hose him down in the back yard." My mom shook her head.

"Dad! You can't hose him down. That's what baby wipes are for." I couldn't believe his ass. Mano was damn near on the floor, laughing his ass off.

"I swear you gone 'cause me to shoot your ass over my son," Mano said to him as he tried to gain his composure.

"Whatever, nigga! That lil' nigga had too much shit going on and I mean that literally. Ion wanna babysit no more. I think his ass did it on purpose." I don't think my dad would have to worry about babysitting ever again.

"Dad, I'm proud of you and Aunt Tay. Mom told me that you both are officially ordained." I smiled at him.

"Yep, and I need y'all to start dressing the part. Y'all can't be out here acting a fool when I'm the man of the cloth," he said that shit like he was serious, and we burst into laughter.

"The man of the cloth? Nigga, you the man of that damn Gucci shirt you got on," Uncle Truth said to him, walking into the kitchen.

"Tru, this is why we've always had a rocky father and son relationship. You should have been teaching me the good book and taking me to church. Instead, yo' ass was teaching me the dope book and taking me to the trap house. God loves you anyway. You did what you had to do, I guess. Oh yeah, me and Tay gone start baptizing people in our pool, if you heathens wanna get saved. I done blessed it and put some holy oil in there so it can cast out them demons in you," my dad spoke and we just looked at him in disbelief.

"Nigga, bring your ass on. I refuse to listen to any more of this shit," Uncle Truth told him. After spending a few more minutes with my mom., we decided to head back to New York. I promised Mano that I would stand beside him every step of the way. If Kemani turns out to be his daughter, I will be there to help him raise her.

Three hours later, we were walking into our penthouse.

"What's that smell?" I asked him.

"I don't know, but it's strong as hell." Mano walked through the house while I went to take the baby into his nursery. Walking into my baby's' room, all I saw was fuckin' red. The odor was so much stronger. His furniture was thrown all over the place and it smelled like bleach. When I got closer to his crib, the scent got stronger. I touched the inside of his mattress and it was drenched in bleach.

"Mano!" I screamed out, and DJ started to cry. I didn't mean to scare my baby, but I was fuckin beyond pissed.

"Yooo, what the fuck!" He roared, walking into the room.

"I don't know who did this shit, but you need to find them! His bed is perfectly made and soaked in some type of bleach. If I would have laid him in that fuckin' bed, it may have burned his skin!" I shouted with tears streaming down my face. I was crying because I was pissed the fuck off.

"Our bedroom is worse. I'm killin' me a muthafucker today! They gone come in our shit and violate us like that!"

He roared, and I took off down the hall to our bedroom. Clothes were all over the place and our bed was destroyed.

"Who the fuck could have done this? It's hard as hell to get up to our penthouse. It has to be someone that works here!" I yelled, walking back to the living room to place DJ in his car seat.

"I called downstairs already; the manager is on his way up. I don't know who decided they wanted to fuck with me and my family. That was the worst decision they've ever made in their life," Mano yelled, kicking the trash can that was by the bar. The doorbell sounded off and I assumed that it was the building manager.

"Mr. Michaels, I don't know how this could have happened. Can you show me where the damages are?" The manager followed Mano to the back, and he was just as shocked as we were.

"Oh no! I can get the cleaning staff up here to get this cleaned up for you. I can alert the authorities and file a report if you would like," he said to Mano.

"Nah, but I would like to see the sign-in book, and any surveillance of visitors coming in yesterday, and today. I also want this shit replaced, I paid too damn much money to live in this building for someone to walk in and just fuck my shit up. They put bleach in my son's fuckin' bed!" The manager jumped because Mano was about to explode.

"Sir, I apologize, and we will do everything in our power to resolve this issue. Please, if you follow me downstairs, we can review the cameras and logbook." This man looked as if he was about to piss on himself, he was so scared.

"Babe, go take pictures of all this shit. We will sleep in one of the guest bedrooms until we can sort this bullshit out." Mano walked out with the manager to look at the cameras.

MANO

I was ready to murder me a nigga! You not gone walk up into my shit like its sweet. I promise whoever did this was gone die, and I mean that shit. I walked into the security room, and the manager asked the security guard to pull the video up from yesterday. It took us damn near two hours to go through the footage, and I saw nobody that I knew or looked familiar.

"I'm sorry, we will look at the employee footage and let you know what we find. I, unfortunately, I can't allow you to look at those tapes. The cleaning staff should already be at your penthouse cleaning the mess up," the manager stated. All I know is they better figure this shit out quick before they ass come up missing. I sent Melani a text to let her know I was running out to go get the baby a new crib. My phone was vibrating, and it was Juelz calling me.

"Yeah." I picked the call up from my car.

"What's up, man? One of the names that you gave us came back. Cassandra Wyatt, she works in the marriage license office. The marriage license for you and Veronica was filed by her. I have some friends down there, and they looked into it for me. Ms. Wyatt is being handled as we speak. I took the liberty of having my attorney start the paperwork to get this taken care of for you. My connect down at the courts will work with him to get this process expedited. Continue planning your wedding, but maybe you should think about getting somebody else to officiate. I want you to be a married man when it's all said and done," Juelz laughed.

"It's official; they both got ordained," I told him.

"I'm telling you this right now, I'm not calling Gabe's ass Rev. nothing," Juelz stated.

"Man, he's already with the shits, so get ready for it. I can't believe that Veronica would do some foul shit like this. Somebody just ran up in my crib and destroyed my shit," I spoke.

"How did that happen? You live in Hudson yard. That place is secured like the White House." He was right, it was impossible to get past the guards in my building.

"I'm going to figure it out," I sighed.

"Let me know if you need us. I will let you know when this is all cleared up for you." Juelz and I ended the call, and I was even more pissed. This bitch has lost her fuckin' mind. I made a u-turn and headed to her house. I pulled up on her block and parked my car. Just as I was getting ready to get out of my car, her door opened up, and some guy walked out. It was damn near dark, so it was hard to see. I hopped out to get a better look at the dude. When he turned to get into his car, I couldn't believe this shit. It was Steven from my damn building, I know this nigga is not fucking with Veronica. I banged on the door, waiting for her to open it up.

"Steve..." I cut that shit short, pushing her ass into the house with my gun pressed to her head.

"Mano! Oh, so you decided to come and see about your wife." She smirked.

"Shut the fuck up, bitch! True enough, at one point, I would have married you in a heartbeat. At one point, I thought you were the one for me, but it turns out that you're a crazy snake ass bitch! We're not married, and we will never be married. Now you got your dumb ass friend into some bullshit she can't get out of. Then you go have a baby and not tell me that there is a possibility that she's mine. I'm getting her tested, and if it turns out that she's mine, you will never see her again. I'm gone let you watch my wife raise her and give her all the things that only a real mother can do. I told you not to fuck with me and you decided to do that shit anyway," I snapped on her ass. This bitch has completely lost her mind.

"You will never get my daughter, her and my mother are long gone. I have them tucked away somewhere nice and cozy!" She smiled, and I had to chuckle and this crazy bitch.

"Nah, bitch, I have them tucked away somewhere nice and fuckin' cozy! Like I said, if she's my daughter, you will never see her. As for your mother. You should be ashamed of the way you've treated her. Your mama is a grown woman and if she wants to continue to deal with you, she can. That's her right, you're her daughter, but if you ever put your hands on her again, I'mma make sure someone put they hands on your bitch ass," I told her.

"Fuck you! I was the one there with you when you had nothing," she cried.

"You were also the one that talked shit because I had nothing. You fucked around on me with other niggas when I had nothing. I was still there trying to save what we had, like a dumbass. It goes to show that pussy can make a mutha-fucka do some dumb ass shit. You talked yo' shit back then; keep that same fuckin' energy and talk your shit now. Because the only woman that will share my life, ride this dick, and spend my money is my fine ass girl waiting at home for me. One last time, stay away from me, and my girl!" I was about to explode on this bitch. I knew it was time for me to go.

"How do you know Steven?" It almost slipped my mind to ask about him.

"None of your fuckin' business, now get the fuck out of my house!" She screamed. I had nothing else to say. I walked out and hopped in my car, heading to get my son's crib. Ten minutes later, I was pulling in the Target parking lot, and my phone was ringing.

"Yeah," I spoke into the phone.

"Mr. Michaels, this is Brian, we know who the person is that went inside your home. His name is Steven Jackson, he was seen going into the penthouse with a woman through the employee service elevators. I'm going to call the authorities and report this on your behalf," Brian stated.

"Nah, you don't have to report it. Listen, I will have to call you back about this later." I hurried his ass of the call; this bitch just signed her death certificate. I knew my dumbass should have put two and two together when I saw his punk ass leaving her house.

Chapter Twenty-Three

VERONICA

I was scared shitless when Mano showed up at my damn door. I thought he found out what I had done to his apartment. At first, I was going to be waiting for him to come home. But when I got inside and saw how he had leveled this bitch up; I was fuckin' pissed. This bitch had clothes and shoes from Fendi, Alexander McQueen, Louis Vuitton, Gucci, and more. All this shit still had price tags on them, and I knew he had got the shit for her. So, I took my anger out and fucked some shit up I there. I even had it out for the fuckin' baby. I didn't give one fuck. Fuck that baby! I can't believe my mama traded on me for that nigga. When I see that hoe, that bitch gone remember who side she supposed to be on. I thought the plan that Cassandra and I put together would work. I dialed my mama phone number.

"Hello." She answered on the first ring.

"When I see you, you're a dead bitch! You took my daughter and handed her over to that nigga." I went off on her ass, and I meant everything I said. I have never hated a person as much as I hated my mother. She was a fuckin' embarrassment. I wanted to be born into a family that had money. I don't know why God allowed her to be my fuckin' mother. Working those dead-end fuckin' jobs and always buying me bullshit secondhand clothes.

"I did what was right, that boy deserves to know the truth. You can threaten me all you want, but if he's her father, I have legal guardianship over her, and I'm signing my rights over to him. I'm going to allow this child to be with a parent that loves and wants her. I knew when you were younger that something was wrong with you. You're a selfish fucked up bitch! I'm not worried about you killing me, because karma is the baddest bitch I know. You will get everything coming to you, and I hope you will ask for forgiveness on your judgment day." This bitch had the nerve to say and hung up on my ass.

"Urrrgggghhhhhhh!" I screamed out loud. Everything that I've planned is falling apart. My ringing phone jolted me from my thoughts.

"Hello," I spoke.

"V, you have to get low. They know it was me that fucked up that nigga's penthouse. One of my homies from work just called to put me up on game," Steven nervously spoke.

"He just left here; he saw you leaving my house. Fuckkkk!

I need you to bring me some money," I spoke, I only had a few hundred dollars left, and that shit wasn't going to get me far.

"You don't need money for the trip you're about to take," a voice I knew all too well said from behind me.

"Mano, how did you get in here?" I had to figure out how I was going to get out of this shit. He walked up to me and snatched my phone from my hand.

"I'm coming for you next, nigga," he calmly said to Steven and threw the phone against the wall.

"Look, I'm sorry. I was just pissed that you moved on and didn't love me anymore." I pleaded with him. He pulled out his phone and dialed a number while his gun was trained on me.

"Yo, I have a messy spill, I'm sending the address to you now," he spoke, ending the call. He screwed a silencer on his gun and my head began to spin, I was so fuckin' scared.

"Please, if you ever loved me, don't do this to me," I cried.

"Bitch, you did this shit to yourself. You can fuck with me all day long, but you fucked up when you decided to fuck with my family. You poured bleach in my fuckin' child's bed! I will never leave room for a bitch to come in and try to harm my family a second time," he roared, as he grabbed me around my neck, choking the life out of me. I never thought that this shit would come back to get me. The way Mano loved me when we were together, I assumed deep down he still did. I guess I was wrong. Tears began to stream down my face as the hold he had around my neck got tighter. The look on his face was something I have never seen before. He placed his gun to my head, pulled the trigger, and everything faded black.

Chapter Twenty-Four

GABE

Gia, Truth, and I were on our way to New York to check on Melani, the baby, and Mano. Melani called her mom and told her what they came home to last night. I immediately called Mano and he gave me the rundown. Whoever this Steven dude is gone see me about my daughter and grandson. It's always some bullshit when you got a delusional nigga or bitch that just can't let go. I don't have a doubt in my mind that Mano loves my daughter. I gave that dude a hard time, but he's proved over and over that he loved her.

"I'm so damn pissed when I see this bitch, I'm beating her ass." Gia was bouncing her legs and texting on her phone.

"Gia, that bitch is expired already! We need to find the nigga she was working with. This is supposed to be a happy time for them, but once again, we have to deal with some bullshit. We all have fought hard as hell to keep our kids safe from shit like this. Now it seems they're dealing with the same type of shit we did back in the day," I told them as we pulled into the parking lot of Mano's building.

"We gone deal with the shit, so that baby girl can enjoy her baby and wedding in peace," Truth said as we signed in to go upstairs. I rang the doorbell and Mano opened the door.

"Hey, what are you guys doing up here? I told you I had it under control, man," Mano said as we walked in.

"Fuck that, we're family and this is what we do. I know you got it, but I'm always gone come when my kids in trouble," I told him.

"Thanks, I appreciate y'all for coming. Let me get Melani." He walked off to go let Lani know we were here.

"I'm always amazed at how beautiful this place is." Gia smiled as she admired their home.

"DJ, look your grandparents are here." Melani smiled, walking into the room with the baby as she hugged and greeted us.

"I'm hungry. Lani, gone in the kitchen and cook yo parents and granddaddy something to eat." I sure hope her ass could cook, 'cause I ain't never seen her boil water at home with us.

"Dad, I'm not good at cooking." She smiled.

"Gia, you need to take her spoiled ass into the kitchen and teach her some shit. How the hell you gone have a husband and can't cook his ass nothing?" I questioned.

"I guess it's a good thing I'm marrying her for love," Mano dumb ass stated.

"Nigga, love can't feed yo' ass at night when that fucking stomach in an uproar. Get her ass some cooking lessons asap," I laughed.

"This y'all house, don't let this nigga tell y'all what to do," Truth said to them.

"Says the nigga that got a whole damn staff over there at the pentagon. The only thing they don't have over at the Baylor estate is a nigga to wipe their ass. I bet that shit is on the horizon though." These niggas had cooks, maids, and security at their damn house. We all fell out laughing, just as the doorbell sounded off.

"That's Juelz, security called and said he was downstairs," Mano said, answering the door.

"Ahhhhh hell, I love it when the crew comes together!" I called Ma, Zelan, and Ju and told them what went down.

"Damn, I didn't think the whole crew was gone come. Kari and Jah, ion really think we need y'all line of work for this shit right here. This some low budget shit to what you two niggas be dealing with." Fuckin' with their ass, this nigga Steven will be hanging upside down from the Statue of Liberty.

"I appreciate y'all for showing up for us like this, but I got this nigga." Mano looked around the room at everybody.

"Chile, we bouts to hang out and when you get the information we need, we gone ride out and find this lil' puss ass nigga. If it wasn't for his ass, that hoe wouldn't have been able to get inside here and fuck with y'all shit. On top of that, they had the fuckin' nerve to try and hurt that lil' precious baby. Ohhhh no, we got something for that ass tuunight, hunty! We play about a lot of shit, but our babies ain't one of them" Ma fussed, and she was right. I think the lil' nigga evil, but his evil ass belongs to us, and I don't fuck around about mine.

"Ma is right. I can't stand a muthafucka that gotta involve the kids just to get to the person you really want. I bet his punk ass let the pussy be the major motivator in helping this bitch. I'm glad to know that you got that thug blood running in yo' veins. You did exactly what should have been done, killed that bitch on sight," Zelan told him.

"To be honest, I was gone let the bitch make it. Faking a marriage to get back at me, and even keeping a child away from me, I was gone let her live. I still don't have an answer on the DNA test yet. Even though I have a strong feeling that little girl is my daughter. When I went to confront her after speaking to Juelz, I saw Steven leaving her house. I asked her about him, and she brushed it off when I said what the fuck I had to say. I left, but when I got the call from the building manager that the fuck boy was the one that came into my shit, I went right back to her shit. Fuckin' with my family is not an option. I will never give another nigga or bitch an opportunity to fuck with mine. I have somebody getting the information I need on him right now. When I get it, he's a dead nigga," Mano said as he poured a drink from his bar.

"I'm riding on this one with you, cuz," Jah told him. Poor Steven was gone get his neck slit before he could blink.

Chapter Twenty-Five

MELANI

I was so glad that my family came up to check on us. When Mano came home last night, he was in bad shape. The anger inside of him had me so afraid to touch him. I knew that he wouldn't hurt me, but I didn't know how to help. At first, I wasn't going to call my parents about what had happened. I knew that no matter what, Mano would handle it and protect his family. But when I saw his condition, I had to call my mom, and I'm glad they all showed up.

"Lani, Dad is right, baby. You need to learn how to cook. I will teach you as we cook dinner for everybody, but we gone get you some cooking lessons."

"I just talked to Toya and she said that Meek is on his way over. She said he has a surprise with him." Grams walked into the kitchen to let us know.

"Lani, baby, where is the best place for us to light up? I need to smoke this blunt," Aunt Cynt asked.

"You can go on the balcony. You will love it out there, it's so beautiful and peaceful," I told her.

"Hell yeah, a blunt sound good as hell right now. One of these days I'mma get y'all to smoke a little of this ganja with our ass. I promise yo' life will never be the same, hunty!" Grams was a mess when it came to her weed.

"Gabe just told me that he and Tay got ordained. Lawwwd, this damn wedding is gone go down in history as the funniest shit ever," Grams said, and my mom was nodding. I had faith in my dad and Aunt Tay. I'm ready to see what they have up their sleeves.

"Yesss, did he tell you they went to church on communion Sunday and Tay was drinking up the people wine, not knowing it was grape juice? Gabe said when they got out of the Church, she had some of the bread pieces to take home to her kids. They acted up in that church," my mom laughed.

"Wheeww chile, they were up in there showing their ass. I sure wish I could have been there to see that shit. I'm going in here to talk about this shit with his ass," Grams said and walked out of the kitchen. We all followed behind her. It made my heart melt looking at everyone just relaxing and having a good time.

"Gabe, why didn't you tell them about you and Tay going to church?" My mom asked.

"Ion know, Gia. They didn't ask if we went to church." My dad shrugged.

"Son, I heard y'all went to church and took communion. I mean, you literally took communion out of the church?" Grams asked my dad.

"Yeah, and it was such a spiritual moment for Tay and I. Ion got nothing to do with the communion bread ending up in my car," my dad said, and everyone fell out laughing.

"Nigga, I know damn well y'all asses didn't go up in Church and take some of their bread? Y'all going straight to hell. How you go in the Lord's house and act a fool?" Uncle Truth told him.

"Tru, we know how we supposed to act in church. Tay only got a couple of pieces to take home for her kids. She wanted the demons out of them, you can't blame her for that. I need to talk to you about some stuff. Since I'm a pastor now, I'mma need you to address me as such. I'mma also need you to come over for bible study on Wednesday nights, and serve on the deacon board," my dad said to Uncle Truth and we were all bent over. My dad was serious as hell, and the look on Uncle Truth's face was everything

"This nigga!" Uncle Zelan said, shaking his head.

"Nigga, really! Bruh, I'm not fucking with you right now. How can you even talk about Church, when yo' ass is the biggest sinner out here?" Truth questioned.

"See, this is the shit I'm talking 'bout. When I try to step out on faith, I always got yo' drug dealing ass to knock my hopes and dreams to the waist side. A parent is supposed to always be there for their children. Teach them and educate them on the ways of the world. Make them better and greater than them. The only thing your ass taught me is how to weigh a kilo and bag up weed. God don't like ugly and you'se an ugly ass nigga!" My dad shouted at Uncle Truth, and Grams damn near broke her neck, getting up.

"Hol up, wayment! This fine specimen of a man ain't got an ugly bone on his body. This nigga even got pretty feet. I think when God created this nigga, he knew what he was doing. I think I can speak for every woman in the US of A, issa fine nigga alert when Truth Baylor is in the muthafuckin' city, hunty!" Grams stated, and I swear my stomach was in so much pain from laughing.

"That nigga don't look that fuckin' good," Uncle Zelan blurted out.

"You just jealous, nigga! Thank you for the compliment, ma." Uncle Truth kissed her on the cheek, and Grams started to shake. I swear this lady was the funniest ever. I doorbell sounded off, and Mano went to answer it. It was Uncle Meek, and I had to blink twice to make sure I wasn't dreaming.

"Well damn! Meek, who the hell is this lil' fine nigga?" Grams asked, as Kari and I made it to the door like we had fire under our ass.

"Josh! OMG, you were supposed to come home a few months ago!" Kari and I both rushed his ass.

"I missed you two as well!" He laughed, hugging us back.

"Ahhh hell, lil' Josh ain't so little no more. I'm just sicka all these fine ass, lil' niggas walking around here. Lawwwd, take me back to the age of twenty-two and sit me right in the middle of the fine nigga convention. Dis jus tew muuurrcch!"

Grams said. She was telling the truth. Josh was definitely nice looking. It has been about four years since we've seen Josh. He enlisted into the military and has been stationed in Hawaii for the past four years.

"Josh, I would like for you to meet my husband, Jah. Jah, this is my cousin Josh," Kari introduced.

"Nice meeting you, I heard a lot about you," Jah said to him.

"Same here, I'm glad she found her happiness. Take care of her," Josh responded to Jah.

"I know it's been a long time since I've talked to you, but I'm getting married in a few weeks, and I just had a baby," I told him, and he just stared at me.

"Wow! That's amazing news. I spoke to Kari a few times, and she never mentioned a thing, other than you were doing fine." Josh glanced at Kari, giving her a weird look.

"Yeah. Babe, this is my best friend Josh. Josh, this is my fiancé Mano," I introduced and I was nervous as hell. Before Josh went away, things with us kind of took a turn when he said that he wanted me to be more than just a friend. I felt like we shouldn't take it there because of the close connection our families had. We did kiss a few times and went on a couple of dates, but that was it. The only person that knew about this was Kari and Aunt Tay. I guess by the way Josh was acting, there were still some underlined feelings for me, but I loved my man, and I would never hurt him.

Chapter Twenty-Six

MANO

"Have you heard anything yet?" Jah asked, walking up to stand by me.

"Nah, I just shot him a text and he said to give him about ten minutes. Once he sends me that, we can be out. The women can stay back and hang out with Melani. What's up with dude? This your first time meeting him?" I asked Jah about this Josh dude.

"Yeah, he seems to be cool. He's been a part of the family since they were little kids. Meek adopted him when he and Toya got married. The three of them were very close from my understanding," Jah stated just as my phone vibrated.

"Let's go, I got an address on ole boy," I said to the guys.

"Y'all need me for this ride?" Meek questioned.

"Nah, go enjoy having your son home. We got this," Zelan told him, and we dapped him up.

"Babe, be careful." Melani wrapped her arms around me, kissing my lips. I could have sworn oh boy chuckled, but maybe I was wrong. I need to make sure I have a lil' talk with my girl about him. We all walked out; Grams and Cynt wouldn't let us leave their ass, so they were with us.

"That's what I'm talking 'bout. A muthafuckin' ride down, I like it when a plan comes together," Grams excitedly stated. The address that he gave was out in Queens. It took us about thirty minutes to get over on that side, and I was ready to kill this nigga. To find out that he was getting close to us just to bring information back to Veronica bitch ass. We pulled up on his street and got out of the trucks.

"I think we should grab him and go. The houses are too close and I don't handle shit when it's like this," Juelz spoke, and I agreed. You never know who the fuck was watching, and it was better safe than sorry.

"Jah, Zelan, and I will take the back and get us inside. We will let you all in as soon as we make it to the front of the house," I told them. I knew without talking to Jah that he would get inside the house. This nigga could get in the White house undetected with his eyes closed.

"Let's do this shit!" Grams yelled, cocking her gun back.

"I called Rell; they will be here in fifteen minutes to pick him up," Zelan stated, and we moved towards the house. Once we got to the back of the house, Jah worked his magic on the lock, and a few minutes later, we were moving inside. We were prepared to move in guns blazing if there was an alarm, but this nigga didn't have one. The downstairs was clear, so Zelan moved to the front door to let the others inside. Jah and I moved upstairs, and we could hear music playing in one of the bedrooms. The guys moved around to check the other rooms out. Zelan and I moved to the last bedroom where the music was coming from.

"Fuckkkkkk, Lani! Fuck this dick, babe!" We heard this nigga say, and Zelan and I looked at each other. My fuckin' blood was boiling, and I have never wanted to kill a nigga so bad in my life. We eased the door open, and this bitch was in bed jerkin' off thinking about my girl.

"What the fuck?!" Zelan yelled, pointing at the laptop on the bed. This nigga was watching a video of Melani and I fuckin' while she was riding me. It was him that was calling her name, but it was my voice on the video feed that he was watching and jerking off to. I fuckin' lost it and jumped on that nigga, beating the shit out of his ass. This bitch has a camera in my muthafuckin' house. It took damn near all of the men in this house to pull me off that nigga. I wanted to break his fuckin' jaw in two. The fuck!

"What the fuck happened?" Gabe asked.

"He has a camera in our house and recorded me and Melani having sex. The nigga was in here jerking off..." Before I could get the rest out, Gabe had jumped on that nigga, and he did this nigga fuckin' dirtier than I did.

"Bitch, you recording my fuckin' daughter, violating their privacy and shit! Trying to bring harm to my grandson. You pussy ass nigga, I will kill yo' ass over my fuckin' kids!" He roared, and I moved to stop him, but Zelan stopped me.

"You gone have to let him rock out! We can't stop him once he's reached this point. Truth will get him; he's the only one that can bring him back."

"Gabe! Bruh, that's enough! Let's get him out here, and y'all can have at his ass soon enough," Truth said to Gabe. I knew I was ready to blow, but I have never seen Gabe like this. All that joking and happy Gabe was gone; this nigga was a fuckin' volcano that already erupted.

"Damn, that nigga got hands!" Jah shook his head and followed them out of the room. Zelan's guys were here, and they pulled Steven out of the room. His ass was barely hanging on, and I need that bitch up to feel everything I had for his ass. It took us about fifteen minutes to get to the warehouse from where we were. Gabe was so mad he hadn't said a word, and I felt every bit of his fuckin' anger. Once we got inside the building, they put Steven in a chair, and he was barely conscious.

"Bitch, wake yo' ass up! You fucked over us for some pussy that didn't want yo' ass to begin with! You came in my house and fucked my shit up to scare my girl and helped this bitch pour bleach in my son's bed, all over his room and clothes! You were better off putting a bullet in me, then to fuck with my child! Then you had the audacity to violate us by putting cameras in my fuckin' house, watching my girl, you bitch nigga!" I roared, punching that nigga dead in his shit. The door to the warehouse opened up, and Lai's men walked in wearing hazmat suits holding some type of liquid in jugs.

"I got a gift for you, baby, but I'm gonna let you finish what you were doing" Grams said to me.

"She begged me to help her. I only helped because I wanted you away from Melani. I helped her during her pregnancy, bringing her food, and going to get medicine because she was sick! You were never there for her; I fell in love with her. With you out of the way, we would have been happy," this nigga Steven gritted out.

"The difference between a man and a fuck boy is that I leave home every fuckin' day, knowing that I satisfied and solidified my place in my girl's life! She's content in what she has at home. I've etched my soul so deep into hers, you could have never penetrated that shit. I will never worry about another nigga taking her from me. The only way that she will get up and leave is if her heart was never in it, to begin with. You see when God created me, bitch, He only created one me. Grams, what you got for me?" I turned to look at her, and her guys walked up, handing me some gloves.

"It's called Mexican stew, pour it wherever you want. This will show him how your baby would have felt if you laid him in that soaked bed filled with whatever he and that bitch put in it," she said as she passed a mask out for everyone to put on. I slid the gloves on and put the mask over my face. When I poured the shit on his legs, the shit melted his fuckin' flesh down to the bone. This nigga screamed so loud; he sounded like a wounded animal.

"Damn! What the fuck you got going on, Lai?!" Zelan

questioned as he moved closer. All I could think about is that I'm never going to get on this lady's bad side.

"Ma, you come up with something every time we get ready to kill a nigga. Most of the shit will make us get the fuck ghost quick, but I like this shit right here," Juelz told her.

"Thank you, son. I got plenty more where that came from." She smiled, pulling up a chair to sit and smoke her blunt with Aunt Cynt. When they said these two ladies were ruthless, there were no lies told. In my eyes, they were the coldest in the game, because they sat there getting high like this shit was a normal thing. I poured some of the liquid right on that nigga's dick!

"That's for having my girl on your mind, bitch!" I spat on that nigga and punched his ass again. He was screaming so much that shit was hurting my damn ears. I began dashing the liquid all over this nigga, watching his body melt right before our eyes, as he continued to scream.

"Yesss, that's how you do it, nephew!" Aunt Cynt laughed, as she passed the blunt to Grams.

"Pop, you can finish him off," I looked at Gabe, and he walked up to him, emptying his clip in his chest. I think the pussy was dead when the first shot entered him, but Gabe and I had something to say, and we said it loud and clear. It was damn near three in the morning by the time we made it back to my place. I took a shower and climbed into bed with my beautiful girl, and held her tight.

I loved this woman, and I would do anything to make sure that she and my son were safe. Tomorrow I planned to take her and DJ over to meet Kemani and Ms. Carol. Even if the results come back and said that Kemani was not my daughter, I wanted to help them. I would talk with Melani more about it tomorrow, but I knew my girl well enough to know that she would want to help. I don't think Ms. Carol will never have to worry about a place to live, how they would eat, or money ever again. It's a shame that Veronica turned out to be the way she was. When I found out that she was abusing her mother, that shit hurt me inside. That lady was so broken about that shit, and all I could do was shed real tears for the hurt she was experiencing.

"I'm glad you made it back to me safe and sound," Melani whispered.

"Nothing will keep me away from you, baby girl. I will always come home to you. I'm sorry that someone from my past caused this bullshit in our lives. I never saw that shit coming, but I can guarantee you nothing like this will happen again. I have some things to talk to you about. We will discuss them later, I'm tired as hell right now."

Chapter Twenty-Seven

GABE

We were heading back to Philly in a couple of hours. I'm glad that we handled that nigga last night, I wanted to rip his fuckin' head from his body. I can't believe that pussy was watching my damn daughter.

"Did you find any more?" I asked Mano. We were going around the house looking for cameras that this nigga set up in here.

"I found two in the bedroom, one in the bathroom, and one in her closet. If we wasn't looking for the shit, we would have never found them." The more he talked, the more his anger showed.

"I just can't believe that Steven would do this shit! I thought he was such a nice guy, but he was a fuckin' lunatic." Lani was shocked and pissed about what we told her.

"After all the shit that's happened, I'm moving my family out of this building. I was going to wait until DJ got a little older, but I need to be in control as to who has access to our home." I couldn't blame Mano. They definitely needed to be in their own private home.

"Trust me, man, there is nothing like your own private space," Truth told him as we were sitting having lunch and watching the news.

"Turn that up. They're talking about that coronavirus," Gia spoke.

"Gia, we don't have to worry about that shit, because it ain't in the US. As far as I'm concerned, they can keep that shit over there. We don't want none of that shit here, ion think I'm ever going out of the country again. I don't want my body filled with nothing, but the holy ghost," I said to her.

"Gia, I don't think we should talk about this, or watch the news." Truth was shaking his head, looking at her all weird. With him saying that shit had me interested in what they were saying.

"Turn it up," I told Melani.

"Jack, it's been reported that the coronavirus has been detected in California and the state of New York. The Governor Of New York has declared a state of emergency," the reporter said, and I jumped up, looking at their ass. They sittin' around like they didn't hear what the fuck that lady just said.

"Ahhh hell nawl! Gia, get yo' shit, and let's get the fuck outta this damn state. Ion feel like getting the Rona all through my body. They said that shit is dropping niggas like flies and I ain't trying to be one of them niggas. What the hell y'all still sitting there for? You better go get yo' shit." They thought my ass was playing, fuck that. Rona won't get my ass. If they're not ready by the time I pack my shit, they asses gone get left.

"Dad, you didn't eat your sandwich," Lani stated, and I looked from the sandwich to her ass.

"Ion really want that, because when I ordered it, I thought it was gone be me and the sandwich. Not me, the sandwich and Rona. The nigga that made that sandwich probably got it and I'm good on that shit." Just as soon as I said that shit, Truth stop chewing and dropped his sandwich back on his plate.

"Mmmmm hmmmmm, yeah, nigga. I thought you would see it my way. Lani, you got some Lysol and sanitizer in here? I'mma need a mask to get the hell out of this building," I told them as I ran to go pack my shit.

"Gabe, are you seriously leaving now?" Gia asked, walking into the room.

"Hell yeah, Gia! Did you not hear what that reporter said? Ion want no parts of that shit. At least we can get home so I can get the house equipped before Rona makes its damn way to Philly. Now bring yo' ass on. You better talk to your daughter and tell them to bring they ass with us. 'Cause if they wait, they gone have to get sprayed down before coming up in our shit," I told her, grabbing our bags and walking back to the living room like I was on a mission.

Truth was already packed and waiting on us, so we could hit the road.

"Dad, I did have a can of Lysol, but I don't have any mask." She handed me the can of Lysol.

"Go get me a white sheet or something. Y'all sho' you don't want to get the hell out of here and come with us?" I asked them.

"Nah, we good. We will see y'all soon," Mano said to us. We hugged them and left out. I wrapped the white sheet around my whole body and started spraying the damn Lysol all the way to the elevator.

"Nigga, can you stop spraying that shit," Truth fussed.

"I'm trying to save our damn life, nigga! I'm spraying this shit until we get to the car. We have to stop for gas, but I think we good until we get into Jersey. You know they will pump the gas for you over there."

When the elevator got down to the first floor, I sprayed Lysol all the way to my damn car. Fuck that, ion feel like playing with Rona or her damn friends, Miller and Heineken. When we made it back, we dropped Truth off at home and picked Layah up. She stayed with Sha and the kids while we were gone.

"Dad, can we go to Five Guys and get a burger?" Layah asked when she got into the car.

"Is that the first thing you say when you see us? With yo' broke begging ass. I guess we can go, 'cause I gotta go to the store and pick up some stuff," I told her. Tay was calling me on Facetime, so I answered the call.

"What up, sis?" I spoke when her face popped on the screen.

"Bro, y'all still in New York?" She asked.

"Hell nawl! I got the hell out of there. They said on the news that the Corona bitch done hit the state of New York," I told her, and this nigga burst out laughing.

"Ohhhh hell to the no! I was gone say we need to figure out when we were going to bring dad down for the wedding. Maybe we should leave his ass where he's at. He might bring that Corona shit to my house, and my damn kids don't need shit else running around inside their ass," Tay said, and we fell out laughing.

"Y'all ain't right. Somebody better go get my father-in-law for his granddaughter's wedding. That's all I'm going to say," Gia said to us, and all of a sudden, Layah ass started coughing in the back seat.

"Mmmmm, mmmmm, this nigga done got the Rona." I grabbed the Lysol and started spraying her ass. I was so busy spraying Malayah's ass, I hung up on Tay.

"Dad! What are you doing? I choked drinking my water. Mom, he sprayed me with Lysol!" Layah yelled with her lips poked out.

"Gabe, stop spraying my damn daughter. She doesn't have the damn virus. I knew I should've listened to Truth and not let your ass watch the news," Gia fussed.

"Gia, you know she works for the devil. You can never be too careful. Next time her ass knows not to get in my car coughing and shit. That shit got me nervous and I ain't taken no chances. I know you're my child, but if you get that shit, you can't stay with me and yo' mama no more." Malayah was mad as hell, and I didn't give not one good got damn.

"Urggggghhhhh." She pouted, and I shrugged. While Gia and Layah went to get burgers, I went into the grocery store and got every damn can of Lysol they had. We gone have Corona kits for every damn body by the time I'm finished.

Chapter Twenty-Eight

MELANI

Kari called and said that Josh wanted to meet up with us for dinner tonight. I didn't see the harm in that. We all were very close, and what Josh and I felt back then was in our teenage years. We're both grown, and I'm getting ready to marry my soulmate. I was still so damn conflicted about going to this dinner, though. I called Aunt Tay because she knew all about Josh and me back then.

"Hey, boo," she spoke when she picked up.

"Aunt Tay, I need some advice. Josh is back home, and he wants to take me and Kari out for dinner before Kari heads back to Georgia."

"Ion know, niece. It might be a trap. That's how the good dick gawds get you. They place a good dick, fine nigga in yo' face, and expect you to walk the faithful line. Especially when you already got a good dick, fine nigga at home. This shit can be all bad. What he look like now? He went into the military, that means he been working out, and he was already fine as hell before he left. Ohhhhh Lawwwwd! He fine fine now, huh?" Aunt Tay questioned and I was laughing.

"We took a picture last night; I'm sending it to your phone now," I told her and texted her the picture.

"Mmmmm, mmmmm, stay the fuck away from this fine ass nicca here. He just looks fuckin' scrumptious. Aht aht, lawwwddd the print in them damn pants. That muthafucka looks like it's ready to burst out and burst into yo' ass. The Good dick Gawwwds did it with this nigga right here! Lawwwd, I may need to pray for your ass and me, for thinking about the shit that's running through my mind right now. Bow yo' head, Lani. Good dick Gawds, me and my niece come to you as a recovering hoe, and a sanctified virgin. Well, she ain't a virgin no mo', but you get my drift, lawwd. We ask that you protect the vajayjay as she sits and breaks bread with this fine nigga from the Good Dick alliance. We ask that you hold her real tight when her shit starts to jump, lawd. I ask that you wipe my mind and place my old fine ass husband back in his prospective place, lawd. Clean my mind from all these young, new, and improved good dick fine niggas you got coming out in 2020, lawd. In all these things we pray in yo' name Gawd! Aman." I was in here hollering from this damn prayer Aunt Tay just did.

"Aunt Tay, you are so crazy," I told her as I continued to laugh.

"Chile, this nigga ain't safe if you do decide to go with

them. Before you go, let that fine ass nigga of yours fuck you so good until he pushes your uterus up there by your heart. That way, you will be relaxed and satisfied. 'Cause if you go up in there with this nigga and lil' baby between yo' legs is hungry, baby. Yo' ass is in trouble!" Aunt Tay laughed, and I swear I was hanging off the bed. I loved talking to my Aunt Tay. She has always kept it real, not to mention she was funny as hell. We talked for a few more minutes and then ended the call. About an hour later, Mano walked into the house, and I decided to take Aunt Tay's advice.

"Sup, beautiful?" He pulled me in for a hug.

"Hey, babe. Did you handle what you needed to handle?" I knew he has been spending a lot of time at home with me since DJ has been born. On top of all of that, we're getting married soon, and there was still so much to be done with that. I'm glad that he's in a position to be home with us more now. This new position has changed everything for him, and I was so happy about that.

"I'm straight, did you mom and dad make it home?" I laughed at his question, because when I talked to my mom, she said my dad is acting a damn fool over this coronavirus.

"Yeah, they're back home. Mom said dad is going crazy over the coronavirus. She said Malayah coughed and he sprayed her with Lysol." Mano and I were laughing so hard tears were falling.

"Yooo, that dude is crazy as hell. He text me asking me if Rona was in my building yet. I said, who the hell is Rona? That nigga sent me a picture of the coronavirus. I didn't even respond to his ass. I swear we all need to have an intervention and get this nigga some help," Mano laughed.

"My mom said they tried that years ago, and my dad told the counselor what they did for a living and that they make people disappear or some shit like that." When my mom told me that story, my dad said they were the ones that needed help.

"I love you, baby girl. I can't wait to spend the rest of my life with you. If I ever do anything to make you feel uncomfortable, you need to let me know. Jah's pop is in town and we're taking our pops to the game tonight." I guess this was a great time to let him know about dinner.

"Yeah, Kari called me earlier about us going to dinner with Josh. I wanted to make sure you didn't have any plans for us before I accepted the invite." He looked at me for a minute without saying anything.

"Tell me about your actual friendship with him. Was it more than a friendship? It was just a vibe that I caught from him that was a little off. I mean, he looked at you a little different, and I had too much shit on my mind last night to address it. Don't get me wrong; I'm not asking if you fucked him because we both know that you didn't." He looked at me, and there was no way that I would ever lie to him.

"We attempted to date a few times, but I didn't want to complicate things. He's like a part of our family. Our parents are too close of friends to create that type of drama. When he went into the military, we agreed to be the best of friends. Of course, he talks to Kari more than he talks to me, and that's why he didn't know about you or the baby. I invited him to the wedding because his parents will be there. If you feel uncomfortable, I will uninvite him." He smiled at me and pulled me closer to him.

"Baby girl, you don't have to uninvite him. I'm never uncomfortable over a nigga, I'm only uncomfortable when my girl makes a move to be unfaithful. I trust you, so I'm not worried about him at all. I just wanted to know the history between you two, other than just having a friendship." He kissed my lips, and I slid my tongue inside his mouth. I would always be hungry for this man, and him alone. I loved every inch of him. Our love was too powerful to allow anyone to come in and destroy it. He pulled my shirt over my head, unsnapping my bra, setting my breasts free.

"You're so fuckin' beautiful." He smiled as he moved his tongue in a circular motion around my nipple and latched on.

"Sssssss," I moaned at the sensation. He lifted from the couch, with me still in his arms and carried me to the bedroom.

"I need you in this big ass bed to fuck you the way I need to right now." The only thing on my mind was him being inside of me. I took off the rest of my clothes and he undressed. Every time I looked at him naked, I creamed on myself. Mano's body was etched in muscles and tattoos. I swear the good man above was careful when he created him. He hit the remote to the surround sound, and *Amazing by Tank* came flowing through. Hovering over me, his beautiful brown eyes pierced through my damn soul.

Taking the head of his dick, he slid it back and forth at my opening and then filled me up. It always took me a few minutes to adjust to his dick. He eased in and out of me as my pussy began to involuntarily pulsate on his dick.

"Got damn, baby!" he groaned as he began to increase his thrust. Digging deeper and deeper into my body as if it was a scientific method to the way he was fuckin' me right now.

"Ohhhhhhh, shit!" I cried out from the amount of pleasure I was feeling. The way he was deep stroking me was becoming overwhelming as tears filled the brim of my eyes.

"Lani, I love every bit of this pussy. Fuck, this shit is too good," he groaned as he pounded on my spot over and over again.

"Manoooo, oh fuck me! Oh shit! I got to pee, baby," I screamed as I felt the urge to pee, and I didn't want to do it on him. That shit would be so embarrassing if that happened.

"Nah, you need to give me that shit!" He growled as his strokes became more powerful and deadly. It dawned on me that I was squirting, this happened to me once before with him. I was unraveling right here in his arms, with tears streaming down my face as cum gushed out of me.

"Fuck, girl! Urgghhhhhhhhh! Ahhhhh shit!" He roared as his cum splashed against my walls so damn hard. It took us a few minutes to gather our composure.

"Who's keeping the baby since we're both hanging out?" He questioned as he kissed my lips and got up, pulling himself out of me.

"Kari's nanny Ms. Rose is going to watch him for me."

"Ok, come take a shower with me. I feel like going another round." He smiled, pulling me into the bathroom with him.

A couple of hours later, Kari, Josh, and I were sitting at Delmonico's steak house in Manhattan for dinner.

"I will be right back, you two. I need to take this call from Miyah," Kari stated and got up to walk up front.

"So, why have you been avoiding my calls? Is it because of this new dude?" Josh asked, looking over at me.

"I had a lot going on, but to be honest, my focus was on my relationship with my fiancé. It wasn't intentional, I'm sorry about that." There was no need to make up some shit about why I didn't answer or call him.

"Melani, I loved you and to come home to see that you're about to get married and have a baby by this nigga is killing me," he expressed.

"Nah, we not doing that. His name is Mano, and we talked about this before you left. There could have never been an us, Josh. I'm truly sorry if your feelings are hurt, I never meant to do that. I love my man, and I will never jeopardize what I have with him. I love you too, but I love you as my best friend. I don't want to lose you or feel uncomfortable when I'm around you. If you can't let this go, then I guess I can't be friends with you. I would hate to lose you as my friend, but if I have to choose, my man will win every time." I genuinely meant what I said to him. This wasn't up for debate. He looked defeated, and I felt bad about that.

"I understand, and I would never ask you to choose. I love

you, and I will move on from this, but don't make me kick your ass. You need to start calling me and answering my calls." He smiled and stood to hug me. A few minutes later, Kari came back to the table, smiling.

"Lani, Miyah told me to tell you, hello and she will see you soon," Kari stated.

"Aww, I'm so glad she's going to be a part of my special day." I knew that Miyah has been busy with the Diamond Clique lately, but I'm glad she had time to be a part of my wedding. We've become closer over the past year, and I cherished our friendship.

"I promise, Josh. I will keep in touch." I smiled at him. For the rest of the night, we got caught up on each other's lives and it felt good to be sitting here with them.

Chapter Twenty-Nine

MANO

It was nice being out with my father, Uncle Chance and Jah the other night. We had a few more days before we all left to go to Philly for our wedding. It seems that everyone was packing up and coming a week before the wedding to hang out and just have a good time. Jah and Kari left today and was headed back to Atlanta for a couple of days. I received a call from Juelz's lawyer, and he told me that everything was taken care of. He sent me some documents, I signed them and sent them back to him.

He said they will be coming in a few days before the wedding. I'm glad Melani and I talked about her friend Josh. I worked closely with Meek, and I didn't want to get into any bullshit with his son over my girl. I haven't had a chance to go over and see Ms. Carol and Kemani in the last few days. I called every day to check on them and she said they were doing fine. I'm not sure if I will tell Ms. Carol about Veronica. In my position, just because a person seems nice, you have to look at shit from all angles. I'm a street nigga, and we don't admit to shit. Telling her I killed her daughter could be suicide in itself for my ass.

"Babe, are you ok?" Melani asked, walking into the room with mail in her hand.

"I'm fine, I was just thinking about Kemani and Ms. Carol. I think we need to get dressed and go over there today. I want you to meet them, I also want to help them in any way that I can if you agree with it." I would never go against my girl, so I'm hoping she is ok with us helping them.

"Absolutely. I'm with you a hundred percent on this. I can't believe that bitch was beating her mother. I wish she was alive, so I could beat her ass again." Lani was heated after I told her all that Veronica had done to her mama.

"I'm happy to hear that. I love you for being so understanding in all of this." I kissed the tip of her nose.

"Here this is addressed to you, I think it's the DNA results. I will let you read this in private." Melani attempted to get out of the bed, but I pulled her back down and opened the letter. I read the results in private, and as I was reading, my blood began to boil. Veronica was an evil bitch to do this shit to me and my daughter. The results say that Kemani was 99.9% my child.

"She's my daughter. I wish I could bring that bitch back to life and kill her ass again for this shit. That little girl went through hell for damn near three years of her life and she didn't have to." I shed some tears because my child didn't deserve to go through the struggles she went through. There is no way that I would have been eating good, and my daughter was somewhere starving.

"I'm sorry this happened to you and Kemani, baby. I know that you hate she went through all of that, but today, her life will change forever. She will never have to go through any of that ever again. Let's get dressed and go see our daughter. I love you, baby." Melani wrapped her arms around me, and the love I had for her surpassed my heart. We got up, took care of our hygiene, and got dressed. We pulled up to my house in Harlem and rang the doorbell. Ms. Carol came to the door, and Kemani was standing behind her.

"Hey, come on in. You could have just used your key to get inside. I was trying to comb this little girl's hair. How are you doing, sweetheart?" Ms. Carol spoke to Melani and we stepped inside. I placed DJ's car seat on the couch between me and his mother.

"It's nice meeting you, I'm Melani." Lani got up and hugged Ms. Carol.

"I've heard so much about you. It's nice to finally meet you and look at this handsome boy." Ms. Carol was admiring DJ. I could only watch Kemani as she sat in the chair across from me, staring at DJ.

"Kemani, would you like to see the baby?" I asked, and she nodded. She was just a baby herself. Ms. Carol said she was starting to talk and form words. She got out of the chair and walked over to stand in front of the baby. She smiled and rubbed DJ's hand, and my heart could barely take it. I picked her up and kissed her cheek, holding her tight.

"Ms. Carol, I got the test results, and she's my daughter." I looked over at her.

"Son, I knew that already. Y ou can look at her and see that she's your daughter. You needed that test for your sanity, and I understand it. I also know that you want her, and I'm willing to sign custody over to you. Just as long as you don't cut me out of her life." I understood how she felt, but I would never stop her from seeing Kemani.

"That will never happen, you will always be in her life," Melani told her, and all I could do was smile.

"She's right, you will always be a part of her life. We would like to do something nice for you, Ms. Carol. You gave your own life and happiness to make sure that you took care of my daughter the best that you could. Melani and I would like to give you this house, and tomorrow morning, I'm going to come and pick you up. I want to open you a bank account up, we're giving you two hundred thousand dollars." I stood to pull her up for a hug. She was shaking and crying uncontrollably.

"Oh my God, the lord is real. I prayed so many nights over this child and to God that he would bless us. I never would have imagined that you would've been our blessing. I'm so grateful to you both," she cried.

"Ms. Carol, I would like to take Kemani with me for a couple of nights. I would like to get to know her and spend some time with her, if that's alright?" I asked her.

"Yes, that's alright with me. I don't think she will give you a problem. She's a good child, and she listens very well. We're still potty training, but she's getting better as the days go by. I will go pack her bag for you," she stated as she attempted to get up.

"All I need is her car seat, I will take care of everything else," I told her.

"Ok, let me go and get that for you." While she was getting the car seat, I picked Kemani up and asked her if she wanted to go with us. She nodded and laid her head on my chest. A few seconds later, she climbed down, walked over to Melani and tried to crawl up in her lap. Melani picked her up, and Kemani started rubbing her hair. That shit warmed a nigga's heart. I think she likes Lani already. Melani finished combing her hair, and Ms. Carol came walking in with the car seat. We got the kids together and left. Kemani didn't cry for her grandmother and was being a big girl for us. We went out to Kings Plaza in Brooklyn and did some shopping for both of the kids. Melani picked out so much shit for Kemani. All I kept hearing her say is, 'awwww babe, this is going to be so cute on her.' I think Melani was going to love the fact that she has a daughter to do girl things with. Once we got all the bags and the kids in the car, we decided to stop and get some dinner.

"I love the feel of this. She's so freaking adorable, and she is taking to both of us so well," Melani smiled, looking over at Kemani.

"Yeah, she is, and I feel like a weight has been lifted that I didn't even know existed. My heart is full. Everything I need is sitting right here in front of me. I hate that things had to end the way they did with her mother because one day, she's going to ask about her. I'm not going to ever lie to my kids about anything. So, I guess when that time comes, we will find a way to talk to her."

"I guess Kemani and I have similar stories, 'cause we both know that I had a father that did the same type of shit to me and my mom. Just know that whatever your decisions are, I'm with you. I know that I'm not her biological mother, but she will never know the difference. I can promise you I will raise her and love her the same way I will with DJ. They will both get the same unconditional love that both a mother and father should give them. Because I'm gone tell you this, nobody can't tell me shit about Gabriel Thomas.

That man did everything for me and gave me a love that only a father could give his child. You would have thought that I was his blood daughter just as Malayah. Don't get it twisted; he loves his daughters, but dad and I just have this unbreakable bond." She didn't have to tell me how much that dude loved her. If I didn't know it, I knew exactly how much he loved her the night we took Steven out.

"Yeah, he does love you for sure." I knew how much Melani loved and respected Gabe.

"I want her to come with us for the wedding. I think she should be a part of our special day." Melani looked over at Kemani and smiled.

"I agree, I will talk to Ms. Carol about it. I know she's my daughter, but for now, I want to kind of include her in our decision making for Kemani," I said to her as we packed up to head home for the night. By the time we made it home, both kids were knocked out. Melani and I got the kids ready for bed. She went to put the baby in his room. I decided to get Kemani situated in her bedroom that we've chosen for her. Both rooms were next door to me and Melani's bedroom. I sat and watched my daughter sleep and vowed to her that I would never leave her. This is a new chapter in both of our lives, but from this moment on, she will always feel loved and be loved. My phone was going off, and it was Quad calling me.

"Yeah!" I spoke.

"Yo, we got the new shipment, and it's going to be disbursed tomorrow. I just wanted to hit you up and let you know it came in." Quad and I have been waiting on this shipment. It was delayed for a couple of weeks, but I'm glad we got it.

"That's good to hear. I got a call from Grange, and he said that they got theirs a couple of days ago out in Cali. I guess I can relax a little and enjoy my upcoming wedding festivities." I was ready for all the shit they had planned for us in Philly.

"Yes, sir. We gone shake some shit up when you hit the city," Quad and I spoke for a few more minutes and ended the call. After my shower, I climbed into bed with my girl and decided to call it a night.

Chapter Thirty

GABE

"Dadddddd!" I heard Malayah scream. She had some friends over and they were outside in the pool. I jumped up to see why she was screaming my name like a crazy person.

"What? And why the hell all y'all standing over in one corner bunched up like that?" I questioned.

"Dad, you have to help us, there is a snake over there crawling on the side of the pool," Layah shouted, and I looked in the direction she was pointing in. It was a big ass snake sitting there like his ass belonged, and ion know what the hell they called me for. I'm not taking my ass out there; they will just be some bit up sucked up damn kids. I shut the door and went to sit my black ass back down on the couch.

"Babe, what is going on? Why are the kids screaming like that?" Gia questioned as she walked into the room.

"Ion even know. They just having fun, I guess." I went back to watching television as if I didn't hear a damn thing.

"Girls, what is going on?" Gia asked them.

"Mom, a snake is over there. I told dad, is he coming to get it?" Layah asked her, and I heard Gia scream.

"Gabe, get yo' black ass up. It's a big ass snake by the damn pool," she yelled.

"Gia, ion really do snakes, and that shit big. That shit might be hungry and try to eat my ass. The kids need to get out of that corner and run their ass in the house," I told her.

"If you don't get your ass up and go kill that shit, I swear you ain't getting no pussy for a year!" Now Gia ass was going too damn far. Why she gotta always bring pussy into this shit? I jumped up and grabbed my phone to call Truth to come help us.

"What's up?" He spoke.

"Tru, there's a snake out by my pool. I need you to come over here and kill it," I told him, but all I heard was the double beep when a call ended. I looked at my phone and that nigga hung up on me. I went outside and found something to kill the snake with. I started to light his ass up, but I didn't want to set my grass on fire, and the fire department had to come out here again.

"Gabe, you were so wrong for that. Got those damn kids scared as hell," Gia fussed.

"Gia, something needs to scare Layah's ass straight. That

lil' heifer always talking shit. Now I'm sorry them other lil' kids got involved, but that's what they ass get for being friends with the devil," I told her and laid my ass back down. Ion know who was gone clean that dead nigga from by the pool, but it damn sure won't be me.

Everything was set and ready to go for the wedding. Tay and I decided that we would say whatever comes to our hearts for the ceremony. My phone started going off and I knew that it was Ma calling. She made me set a ringtone for her of *Pills & Automobiles by Chris Brown.*

"Ma, what's up?! I said, answering the phone.

"I have a surprise that I want to add to the decorations for the beautiful couple. I don't want anyone to see until it's time to go in for the wedding. It's going to be delivered and set up the night before, so tell Gia to make sure everything is complete," she stated, and I could only imagine what the fuck she had going on.

"Alright, I will let her know. What time y'all coming down tomorrow?" I asked her. All of the guests for the wedding is coming in a week early. We all wanted to hang out and have some family fun.

"We're leaving in the morning; we should be there by noon. You know the entire family is coming, so we got to get all these niggas packed up around here. Juelz and Ciera are staying with Truth and Shanice, and the rest of us will be staying with you and Gia."

"Yeah, put all the bougie rich niggas in the same house.

This the party house over here, but I'mma tell y'all now, you gone have to get sprayed down before you come up in here.

Y'all state got the Rona, and I heard this morning there may be a case in Philly, and other states now. I got Rona kits for everybody when we go out," I told her ass. I'm not playing about that shit. Errrbody getting stopped at the front door.

"Chile, I'm not fuckin' with you, but I feel you. Juelz done had the doctor and his team come out to check all of his family. So, we were screened for it. Maybe y'all should do the same thing. 'Cause Lai ain't got time for that shit," Ma laughed.

"You know that's a good idea. I'm gone talk to Truth about it," I told her. We talked for a few more minutes before ending the call. Gia came in and sat down beside me, and that ass was looking good as hell.

"Gia, come give me some ass before all the guest gets here. You know you be screaming loud as fuck, and everybody in the house gone know we been fuckin'." I smiled at her, and she rolled her eyes.

"Gabe, your ass is not gone hold out for a week with no pussy. I just gave yo' ass some this morning, and my girl still hurts from that shit. That'll be a hard no for me right now." I frowned because I don't say no to her ass when she's begging for my shit in public.

"Gia, I'm not playing with you." My shit was rock hard, and she was the only one that could help me with that problem.

"Ok, on one condition," she said to me.

"What's that?" She sat with a smirk on her face and my ass was ready to go upstairs.

"I will give it to you, but I want to have another baby. So, when we go upstairs that's what we gone do, make another baby." She clapped and started gyrating in her seat.

"Who?! Hell nawl! Mmmmm mmmm, you only birth evil ass kids, and ion want no more them. I told you I can't have no more kids anyway, I got my shit fixed." She made my damn dick go down. I know everybody be wanting to have kid after kid when they in love and get married and shit! But that just ain't us. When that lil heifer, we got upstairs came out, she ruined it for my ass. In my mind, every kid in America is evil, and I'm watching all them lil' fuckers when they around me. Truth and Sha over there having badass baby after baby. As for me and my house, ion got time for that shit over here.

"Gabe, stop it. You know we can have one more," she laughed.

"Fuck that, Gia! We in our mid-forties. By the time the baby goes to middle school, yo ass gone be walking with a cane. Ion even want the pussy no more, and I know you said that shit because you knew I wasn't gone want it. Slick ass heifer, but as soon as I get my mind right, we fuckin'." Her slick ass wasn't fooling me. I'mma be balls deep before the night was over with. She laughed and walked out of the room. I had some runs to make before everyone got here in the morning, so I headed out to handle my business.

Chapter Thirty-One

MELANI

I was so excited to be home; this was it the week that we have all been waiting for. Our wedding was this coming weekend, and we just pulled up to my parent's house. This moment meant so much more to us because we had Kemani with us. Not only did we bring Kemani, but we decided to invite Ms. Carol to come with us.

"Damn, it's a lot of trucks out her. I guess the crew has made it. I will come back for the rest of the bags. Y'all, come on," Mano said to us as he got DJ out of the car. When we opened the door, my dad came sliding down the hall fast as hell, with his hands up.

"Hold up! I need you to hand me the baby and y'all walk in one by one," he spoke, and I looked at Mano. We both knew he was up to some shit, but I handed the baby off anyway.

"Lawwwd, this nigga at it again." Grams came walking up

laughing. I walked through first, and some shit sprayed out as I walked through the door.

"What the hell? Man, what was that? I don't want shit spraying on me," Mano laughed, and Ms. Carol was looking nervous as hell.

"Nigga, it's safe, but you gone have to trust me and get yo' ass sprayed or you and Rona can stay y'all asses out the door!" My dad told him, and I was cracking the hell up. I didn't notice the gloves on his hands. When I first came through, he wouldn't hand over my baby. He said he had to get sanitized first. I just shook my head at my dad.

"I guess if it's safe, I will walk through it." Ms. Carol shrugged and walked on through as she got sprayed.

"Ms. Carol, it sure is good to see you and this pretty lil' girl here. Now step back, so this nigga can come through, and he a street nigga I think we need to spray his ass twice," my dad said as he and Grams were in a fit of laughter.

"I'm a distro, it's a difference, nigga!" Mano told him as he walked through, and the shit came sprayed down on him.

"Uhhhh, whatever you want to tell yo'self! You sell drugs just like the street nigga. The only difference is yo' thug ass sell it to his ass, and he turns around and sells it on the street. The bottom line is both you niggas sell drugs on the streets and off it! God can change yo' life it you let him. All you got to do is open your heart and come," my dad said, and we were confused and on the floor in laughter.

"This nigga! Bruh, are you doing an altar call in your doorway?" Zelan questioned him.

"Z, you don't have to be in church to come to God. Church is wherever you decide to praise him! Dang, you can tell who the heathens are in this family," Dad said, and walked off with our baby.

"Where are you taking my son?" Mano asked him.

"I'm going to clean this Rona off his ass, and then y'all can have him back," he yelled out.

"Somebody better go get that baby. That nigga might be giving him a Lysol bath," Uncle Zelan stated, shaking his head.

"I will go and get him," my mom said as she hugged us and walked off to go find my dad. We walked into the kitchen, I introduced Ms. Carol and Kemani to the family, and they welcomed them both with open arms.

"Carol, hunny, you have to get in where you fit in around here. We drink, we get high, and we acts the hell up. I promise before it's all said and done, you will have a good time with this crazy ass family. We love hard and will kill your ass if you cross us. Don't cross us, baby, but welcome to the family," Grams said to her, and I was so damn embarrassed.

"Lani, you ready for y'all party? Wheeewww chile, I got some surprises for y'all. We gone tear Philly the hell down, they gone read about us in the morning paper. Girls gone wild the Lai edition, we gone make a movie by the end of the night. I don't know what the hell you guys gone be doing." Grams was making me nervous, but I'm here for it all. We decided that we would all party together. Mano didn't want the normal Bachelor party nor did I want a bachelorette party. So, we all decided to go out and celebrate together.

"Ma, don't come with no bullshit," Uncle Zelan said to her.

"Nigga, that's like telling her to stop smoking weed. It's never gone happen," Uncle Meek spoke as he, Aunt Toya, Josh, and Sanai came into the kitchen.

"Hey, everyone. Sanai, you're getting so big and beautiful as ever with those purple eyes of yours," I said to her.

"Thank you. Where is Layah?" She questioned, and I haven't seen Layah since I've been here.

"I'm not sure. Go check the family room, and if she's not in there, go up to her room. When you go upstairs, make a left, and she's the double door at the end of the hall." My mom and dad had Layah so spoiled. When dad got this house, and we moved in, Layah was so upset that she didn't have a double door like mom and dad's room. So, Dad had the contractors come out and install a double door for Layah's bedroom. She even had a small sitting room area, because she wanted it to look just like their bedroom. Layah and Dad argued, but she had him wrapped around her fingers very tight. My dad ordered food, and the family partied until the wee hours of the morning.

By the time I got up, it was damn near lunchtime, and the family was all up having lunch. Mano was actually laughing and talking with Josh, and Ju Ju, and that made me happy.

"Does anyone know what time Kari, Jah, and Miyah are coming in today?" I asked.

"They're already here, they are over to Truth's house. She said they would be here in an hour; they had to drop the baby off to Ciera. She wanted to spend time with her grandbaby," my mom spoke as she fixed me a plate. About twenty minutes later, Kari, Miyah, and Jah came into the house, and Jah was laughing so damn hard about my dad's spray machine.

"Yoooo, that dude is my dude for sure. Gabe ain't playing no games with none of y'all asses," Jah stated as he sat at the table.

"None, but you gotta love his crazy ass," Mano laughed, giving his cousin dap. "Laniiii, it's almost time." Kari excitedly hugged me.

"Hey, sis. You ready to get our party on?" Miyah asked as she hugged me.

"I'm ready." I was ready to see everyone act up because I knew it was gonna happen.

"Ohhhhh, if Miyah is going, somebody has to get me in. I want to see her bounce her booty all around," JuJu said, and Grams popped him in the head.

"Boy, sit yo

dumb ass down and tuck that lil' pencil back in yo' zipper. You not ready, young snapper!" We all fell out laughing, Grams was a damn fool for that one. Josh was staring at Miyah, and Kari must have caught it because she introduced them.

"Josh, this is my best friend Miyah, and Miyah, this is my cousin Josh that I'm always talking about." She smiled, and they both greeted each other.

"Miyah, girlll, you might want to hop on and take a ride, chile! 'Causeee, babby, look a here. In my younger years, I would of...Oop never mind!" Grams swatted her hands and went to pour a drink.

"I feel you, Lai. It's something in the water that got their ass looking like that," Aunt Cynt said and they fell out laughing.

"If y'all don't stop drooling over my damn son," Uncle Meek told them, kissing both ladies on the cheek.

"If you don't get yo' lil fine ass away from us, we might drool on you! Sorry, Toya, he left it open for me to say that shit." Grams and Aunt Cynt fell out laughing. Aunt Toya just shook her head, because she knew they were always playing with the guys like that.

"Did Uncle Daniel get here yet?" Jah questioned.

"Yeah, he's at the hotel with his new girl. He's going to meet us at the club tonight." I knew Mano was super excited about his dad meeting someone. I was happy for my father in-law. He deserved happiness.

We were sitting in the VIP section of the X Lounge, which is owned by Truth and another friend of ours. The party was in full swing, and everyone seemed to be having a good time. We had the entire VIP section closed off and our own personal DJ up here.

"Babe, you really outdid yourself putting this all together for our baby." Gia ass was feeling tipsy, and tonight it was bound to go down anywhere we decided to get it in at.

"I will do anything for my daughters. I'm proud of Lani. She stood her ground and fought for the love she had for Mano. To be honest, I'm glad she chose him, he's a decent dude. But don't tell his ass I said that shit," I laughed, kissing her lips.

"Alright, everyone, I need for you to get ready! We got some shit for the bride and groom!" The DJ announced. *Show*

Me Love by Alicia keys Ft. Miguel came blasting through the speakers, as a male and female dancer came out dancing together. Dancers were swinging from ropes out of the ceiling; this was some shit we've never seen before. This shit was crazy as hell in here. The male dancers disbursed and started dancing in front of the women. The women dancers did the same thing to the men, but these damn women seem to be having too much fuckin' fun.

Ma was passing out money and when I tell you they ass was making it rain, drizzle, and thunderstorm over these niggas. She gave our asses money as well, but the only person throwing the shit was Mano and Jah slow asses. The one male dancer got up in Ari's face, throwing his shit on her ass, and she was so damn drunk, she was into that shit. Zelan was made it to that side of the room before you could blink good. The rest of the guys decided to let the girls rock out and have some fun just as long as there was no touching. The guys did the same thing, but the difference for us is we didn't want the dancers. It was good enough to watch our wives dance and have fun. That is until my ex-stripper damn wife decided that she wanted to bring out some of her old moves. I almost broke my damn neck getting up out of that fuckin' chair. Gia's looks and body haven't changed at all. If anything, her body enhanced. She was beautiful, and still fine as hell. I be damn if she was gone be bouncing that shit around for the next nigga, hell nawl!

"Gabe, what's wrong? What happened to letting the ladies

have a good time?" Truth, Quad, and Zelan stopped me, asking dumb ass questions.

"Fuck all that! She is supposed to be the first lady. How the hell she gone be the first lady during the day and Diamond the pussy popper at night? Hell, to the nawl!" I told them, moving fast as hell to get to her ass. All you could hear is them niggas laughing, but I didn't give a damn. Tay, and Tammy ass was cheering her on and throwing money on her ass until they saw me coming.

"Get it, get it!" Tammy ass yelled.

"Giaaaaaa, runnnn, bitch! Lawwwwd, the good dick gawds done sent my brother to fuck you up!" Tay yelled out. Gia ass stopped dancing and turned to look in my direction.

"Heyyyy, baby! This party is off the chain and I'm horny as hell."

"Gia, get yo' ass over on that couch and sit the fuck down! You out here throwing yo' shit like you the headliner about to hit the stage at Magic City," I went off, and she burst into laughter gyrating her ass all on me.

"I still got it, boo, and I'mma give you all this good pussy when we get home," she laughed, as Ma and the ladies cheered her on. These damn women were fucked up, and all I could do was shake my head at their ass. I thought Truth and Sha's asses were getting ready to fuck right here in VIP, the way they were carrying on.

"Yesssss, Cynt, you got all this good shit?" Ma asked her.

"I got all the juice, Lai!" Aunt Cynt said as she smoked on her blunt.

"I told their asses; this shit was gone be a movie," Ma laughed, giving Cynt a high five.

"Lai, we got any more brownies or did the girls eat them all?" Aunt Cynt asked, and I looked around at all of the ladies. These niggas were high and drunk! No wonder they ass was on one tonight, including my damn daughter.

"Babe, come go out to the car with me." Gia climbed in my lap, rubbing on my dick and shit.

"Gia, sit yo' high ass down. I will take care of you when we get home," I said to her. This girl started grinding her shit on my dick, and my dick rose to the attention quick as hell.

"Come on, babe. I need some and I need that shit now," she moaned in my ear. I made her get up and pulled her ass right out of the club. I turned the car on and climbed into the back seat, pulling my shit out. She lifted her dress, pulling her thong off, climbing into my lap, and easing down on my dick. I don't know if it was the weed or liquor, but damn, the way this pussy was gripping my dick, it had my ass ready to bust.

"Shitt! Mmmmmm, this feels so fuckin good," Gia moaned as she stuck her tongue inside my mouth. Our asses were so horny we didn't give a damn about being outside.

"Damnn, Gia! I'mma about to bust...Ahhhh, fuck!" I growled as she started bouncing on my shit.

"Fuckkk! I'm cumming, babe! Ohhhhh shit!" She screamed so loud; I just knew them niggas in the club heard her. I gripped her ass and started drilling the shit out of her, and a few minutes later, we both were cumming together.

"That was our baby right there." This nigga said, and I wanted to gut punch her ass and throw her out the window.

"Gia, get yo' high ass off me. You fuckin' up the whole damn experience," I told her, and she burst out laughing. We cleaned up with the wipes that she had and decided to leave them niggas in the club and go home.

A few days had past and it was the day of the wedding. Tay and I were in a holding room, going over what we were going to say. The shit was supposed to come from the heart, but we wanted to be on the same page.

"Bruh, give me another shot, I'm nervous as hell," Tay said, and I poured her another shot of Henny.

"Ion think we supposed to be getting drunk, Tay, and we done had too many of these damn shots." The liquor was flowing, and I was good and ready.

"I know we gotta put this shit up. We just gonna go out there and do us," Tay spoke, just as her cousin, Love walked into the room.

"Are you two ready for your debut? I can't believe you two are really doing this. This is dope and makes me damn nervous at the same time. Wait, are you two fools in here drinking?" She asked, and Tay and I burst into a fit of laughter. I think we were both fucked up, but we were going to give them the best wedding ceremony ever.

Chapter Thirty-Three

MELANI

I arrived at the venue a couple of hours ago and I was so freaking nervous. Today I was going to marry the man of my dreams. I loved Demano with every part of me, and to have our children here to be a part of this day was everything to me. Kemani looked absolutely beautiful in her little dress. We tried to get a dress that matched mine, but she was still a little baby herself. My bridesmaids were stunning, and so was my mother. Mano and I decided that we wouldn't have a side for the groom and one for the bride. We wanted everyone to spread out and sit together.

Our family was about togetherness and being blended, and that's how it would be with Mano and his father. They had a few cousins, and close family friends that came in for the wedding and I was very happy about that. He would never have to worry about having a mother because I'm sharing my mother with him, and she was proud to take the position. I loved the relationship they had with each other. My mom and grandmother walked into the room, and I swear they looked like twins. My grandma was aging well, and I loved her so much. I was kind of hoping that my biological dad's mom could have had the same type of relationship, but that's behind me now.

"Lani, you look amazing," my grandma spoke as she hugged me.

"Thank you, Grandma." I smiled, and kissed her cheeks.

"You look beautiful, baby. I just saw my son, and he looks so handsome. He said he's ready to get married." My mom had tears in her eyes.

"Lani, we have to take some more pictures before the wedding starts. They said we have about thirty more minutes," Kari stated. We got all the photos that we needed, then I took some pictures with Kemani and DJ. My son was so adorable in his little suit. The kids and Ms. Carol were going to be with my mom and dad for a few days while Mano and I go on a quick little honeymoon getaway.

"Ahhhhh, what a beautiful girl you are," my dad said, walking into the room.

"Hi, daddy. Thank you." I smiled at the man that showed me how a man is supposed to love a woman. The way he loved his wife and daughters is the way that I wanted my husband to love me and my children. I appreciate everything he has done in my life.

"I love you, beautiful. I think you made a good choice in

Mano, to have as your husband. I'm not going to give you a long drawn out speech, but you know the love I have for you as my daughter will always be unconditional. I know I may drive you, and Layah crazy, but everything I do is for you." He kissed me, and the tears I have been trying to hold in started to fall.

"I love you so much, dad." I wrapped my arms around him so tight.

"Ok, Uncle Truth is going to come and get you, and I will be waiting for you to walk you down the aisle," he said, kissing my cheek and leaving the room. Someone knocked on the door, and I went to answer it, thinking it was Uncle Truth. It was my makeup artist coming to touch me up.

"Melani, the groom sent this letter and gift for you." She handed me the box and letter, and I read it.

My beautiful lady, I can't wait to see you walk down that aisle. Melani, the love that I have for you is much deeper than you know. I don't just hold you in my heart, I carry you in my soul. You exude everything that I could have ever imagine for me as my wife. I knew the day I met you, that you would have my children and be my wife. Our hearts beat as one, and our souls have collided. You are the beautiful creation the God molded just for me. I will always breathe life and love into your spirit, mind, body, and soul. You will forever be safe with me- Mano

I was a fuckin' mess. That man was everything, and my heart was so full. I opened the box, and he sent me a beautiful diamond bracelet. The makeup artist helped me put it on, and she touched up my makeup. In just a few more minutes, I would be Mrs. Demano Michaels.

MANO

We were standing outside of the room where the ceremony was being held. Grams said she had a surprise for us, and we were all waiting to see what it was. I knew it was going to be some crazy shit, and I had to prepare myself for it.

"Bruh, stop pacing, and take this drink." Jah walked up to me, handing me a drink.

"I'm good. You got the ring, right?" Melani didn't know it, but I changed her ring out and got something a little bigger.

"Yeah, I got the ring, and everything is going to be fine," Jah stated, patting me on my back.

"Okkkk, everyone, Trixie, and I would like to make an announcement. We're about to open the doors, but I have to give one housekeeping rule. Do not say the word shoot. I repeat, do not say the word shoot in this room, and everybody will be fine and come out alive!" Grams stated, and Trixie ass was shaking her head in agreeance and passing out blunts to all the guest. *What the fuck these two had going on?*

"This shit is about to be a hot ghetto mess. These niggas passing out fuckin blunts as favors." Zelan shook his head, and I swear I was starting to rethink this entire damn decision. They opened the door, and everybody was standing there peeping inside. It was as if nobody wanted to walk in the damn room. Zelan, Meek, Jah, Quad, and I walked in, and the first thing we noticed is the damn spray that was coming from every damn direction. We knew that Gabe's ass had everything to do with that shit. But the shit that took us out was that monkeys were hanging from the ceilings with tuxedos on. Some were in white cages holding Ak's, and some were on swings playing the violin. The fuckin violin and I promise you we fuckin' lost it. Tears were streaming down my damn face, I was on my damn knees in these people shit. I have never laughed so hard in my entire life. My gotdamn chest was hurting at the bullshit we were witnessing. All of a sudden music came on, and Gabe and Tay were two-stepping down the aisle to *Boo'd Up by Ella Mai*. They had everybody in this bitch partying, and the wedding hadn't even started yet.

"What kind of wedding is this?" Ju Ju asked.

"Nigga, you just worry about walking yo' ass down the aisle," Grams told him.

"This is going to be the shit show of the fuckin' century." Truth was shaking his head and we all fell out laughing again.

"I have to get me a damn drink. These niggas two-stepping and we can't say the word sho..." Zelan stopped talking and started looking up at the damn ceiling.

"Bruh, watch what you say," Truth laughed.

"Man, I'm too damn gangsta for this shit. If them niggas start bussin', I'mma blow they ass to monkey heaven, and that's a muthafuckin' fact. Now I'm going to get me some liquor until this shit starts to make sense or becomes funny as hell! Whatever comes first, I will be cool with it." Zelan walked away, shaking his head and went to grab a drink from the outside bar.

"I'm going with you, 'cause this shit is crazy," Quad laughed.

"Oh my God, I had no idea that she was doing this. I can't stop laughing," Gia said as she walked up to us. I looked around. The place was beautiful; these damn monkeys were ready for whatever, but they blended right in.

"Excuse me, we gone need y'all to take a seat so we can get this show on the road. Y'all know gawdddd is good," Aunt Tay yelled, and the guests was shaking their heads in agreeance.

"Yes, lawwd! He is my way maker. Thannnk ya Jesus," Grams yelled out.

"Lawwwd, we got a room full of drug dealers. They don't know how good God is. Well, I take that back; they should really know how good he is, 'cause they asses sittin in here," this nigga Gabe said, and I was doing my best to hold in my laughter. Truth put his hands over his face shaking his head.

"You better say a word, brother!" Tay shouted. This shit was downright hilarious.

The men that were a part of the wedding stepped out of the room and took their places. I walked up to take my place beside Gabe and Tay. *Why I Love You by Major* started playing, and the ceremony started. Kemani came down the aisle with her basket of flowers, but she didn't throw any on the floor. My baby was not feeling all these people, so the planner took the flowers and helped her. Truth escorted Gia down the aisle, Gabe's father escorted Gia's mother down the aisle, and they were both stunning. Melani was so excited about her grandfather being here. Zelan escorted Ari in, Juelz Jr. escorted Miyah in, and Jah escorted Kari down. Malayah walked down the aisle by herself, and she was so beautiful.

I was getting nervous because it was time for me to see my girl, and I had a surprise that was going to shock her and the family. The only people that knew about this were Jah, my uncle Chance, and my pops. The planner pushed a keyboard out in front of the aisle with a microphone attached, and I stepped down to take a seat.

"Nigga, what are you doing? I hope yo' ass ain't about to embarrass us, and we just let you in the family," Gabe whispered, and I chuckled.

"Ohhhh Lawwwd! Good dick Gawds, this how you're doing it now. The alliance is coming with some type of talent! Wheeewww, Sin ass would have got me at the first note if that nigga would have sung to me back in the day. My ass would have been all types of crazy, and my cousin Love too. Well, you can't get no worse than what she is right now." The crowd burst into laughter after hearing Tay go on and on. Gabe left the room to get Melani, so he could escort her down the aisle. Singing and playing the piano was just a talent that I picked up when I was a teenager. I just never did it in front of anyone other than my family.

This would be the first time that Melani would hear me sing. I started playing, and the song *You by Jesse Powell* flowed out of my mouth. When Melani and Gabe came in, and she noticed that it was me singing, she threw her hands over her mouth, and the tears started flowing for both of us. I continued to sing until the song was over. I stood waiting for Gabe to give me her hand. This woman was fuckin' amazingly beautiful, and I wanted them to hurry this shit up.

"Who gives this woman to this man?" Tay asked as she looked at us.

"Tay, why the hell you gone ask that dumb ass question when I'm standing right here?" Gabe questioned her, looking crazy as hell.

"Huh? This nigga slow," Zelan blurted out.

"Nigga! That's what you supposed to ask. Just say I do and get yo' dumb ass up here," Tay fussed, and that special moment we just had was replaced with my damn side hurting.

"Mano and Melani, God is your rock. When you feeleth trouble, you look to him and he will provide the desires of your heart," Gabe shouted.

"Nigga, is feeleth even a word, and why is you hollering?" Zelan asked, shaking his head.

"We tired of standing up here. Lani, I know the Gawds of the alliance sent this here man to you. They got you already, and I pray that you stay sane through this marriage. Give them the rings, please. Lani, do you take Demano from the alliance to be your husband?" Tay asked her.

"I do." Melani smiled, looking up at me.

"Demano, do you take my daughter to be your wife? Do yo' ass promise to protect her, love her, and save her from Rona? Do you promise me that you will provide for her, and make sure she never calls home for money? Because after today, I'm broke, and once I give her to yo' ass, I don't want her back. Do you take her to be your wife?" I was trying to gather myself to answer this nigga, 'cause his ass is really crazy.

"I do, man," I responded.

"Ok, y'all married. Gone and kiss your bride and make that shit quick; we need us a drink."

A few minutes later, Melani and I were husband and wife. It was truly a crazy ass wedding, and the pastors got tired of talking, but I enjoyed every minute of it. We didn't want it to be like every other wedding. It was perfect enough for us. Melani and I spent a few minutes together while everyone went outside to the grounds for the reception.

"All I got to say is congrats, and I pray to God that y'all asses is married," Grams laughed, as she hugged us.

"Congratulations, babies! I second what Lai just said. Now it's time to smoke and party." Aunt Cynt pulled her blunt out, and she and Grams walked out to the reception.

"I love you, Mrs. Michaels." I kissed her lips.

"I love you back, baby. Why didn't you tell me that you

could sing? You sounded just like his ass. Make sure you sing to me tonight when you're deep inside me." She wrapped her arms around me, and I latched onto her lips.

"I promise, we gone be singing together all night long, shawty." This woman was truly my better half.

"I'm proud of you, son and Melani, welcome to the family. I've always wanted a daughter, and now I have a beautiful one." My dad smiled, and Melani gave him the biggest hug.

"Thank you, pops." I was happy that he was able to witness his only child get married. We walked out to the reception after we took a few pictures, and the party was in full swing. I was blessed, and I thank God for granting me a beautiful wife, and my kids. I will forever be grateful for the gift that he's given to me.

The End

GET CONNECTED WITH AUTHOR K. RENEE

To get VIP access of new releases, and sneak peeks please join my mailing list.

Text KRENEE to 22828

Website www.authorkrenee.com

Facebook: https://www.facebook.com/karen.renee.9421450

Instagram: http://www.instagram.com/Authorkrenee

www.ingramcontent.com/pod-product-compliance
Lightning Source LLC
Chambersburg PA
CBHW061449150726
47987CB00001B/391